C000136505

WOLF'S MIDLIFE SECRET CHILD

MARKED OVER FORTY

MEG RIPLEY

SHIFTER NATION

Copyright © 2023 by Meg Ripley

www.authormegripley.com

All rights reserved. Printed in the United States of America. No part of this book may be used or reproduced in any manner whatsoever without written permission except in the case of brief quotations embodied in critical articles or reviews.

This book is a work of fiction. Names, characters, businesses, organizations, places, events and incidents either are the product of the author's imagination or are used fictitiously. Any resemblance to actual persons, living or dead, events, or locales is entirely coincidental.

Disclaimer

This book is intended for readers age 18 and over. It contains mature situations and language that may be objectionable to some readers.

CONTENTS

WOLF'S MIDLIFE SECRET CHILD

WOLF'S MIDLIFE SECRET CHILD

MARKED OVER FORTY

1

"UGH! HOW CAN ANYONE ACTUALLY WEAR THESE?"

Sarah allowed a glimmer of a smile to cross over her face as she looked at her daughter holding out a pair of men's bikini briefs by its string. Ava may not know much of the outside world, but she was still just as much of a sixteen-year-old girl as she'd be in other circumstances. "I've yet to figure that out, honey, and frankly, I don't want to. At least we have the luxury of a washing machine and dryer instead of doing it by hand like people had to back in the day."

Ava glared over her head as someone stomped through the Greystone packhouse on the floor above them. "I don't know. There might've been some benefits to that."

"Yeah? Like what?"

Her daughter rolled her shoulder as she poured detergent into the washing machine, keeping her head back as she chucked the manties into the machine. "Well, maybe not if I had to wash a load of *these*, but I don't know. Doing it outside, I guess?"

Sarah pulled the next shirt from the basket at her feet and laid it carefully over the ironing board. The dryer beeped, letting her know the towels were done. "Are you really going to tell me you'd rather touch all these dirty clothes with your hands while you scrubbed them in filthy water against a washboard?"

Moving aside the next load of dirty laundry, Ava gagged. "Never mind, you're right. I just don't see why the people in this packhouse can't wash their own clothes."

Sarah had no answer for that. Her mouth hardened into a grim line, knowing Ava wouldn't have these kinds of responsibilities if it weren't for her. Sure, she'd be expected to do chores. Sarah knew she'd never let any child of hers just run around with all the freedom in the world and no responsibility. Ava had the opposite, and there was nothing Sarah could do about it.

"Sarah!" The thundering footsteps overhead were now thundering down the basement steps, sending bits of dust shaking down from the old wooden boards and making the mason jars in the storage space rattle.

Her stomach tightened, and she felt her shoulders hunch up around her ears, but Sarah forced them back down again. She wouldn't let Edward know what he made her feel whenever she saw or even heard him. He had enough power, and she wouldn't give him a shred more of it. "Yes?" she asked, pointedly focusing on her ironing as she created a perfect crease down one sleeve.

"Where's my blue shirt? The button-down one? You said you'd have it clean before tonight." Coming around from the stairwell and into the laundry area of the basement, Edward Greystone glowered at his daughter as he put his fists on either side of the belly that lapped his belt.

"It's right here, as promised." Sarah set down the iron and lifted the blue shirt in question from the nearby rack. "I even got all those grease stains off the front. You should be more careful the next time you decide to gorge yourself on bratwurst."

He snatched it from her grasp. "Don't try to

lecture me. You just turned forty. You ought to know your place in this pack by now."

Giving him a mock smile and wide eyes, Sarah tented the fingers of one hand over her collarbone. "Oh, you remembered! I thought you'd forgotten today was my birthday. Is that why you wanted your best shirt? So we could all go out to dinner and celebrate? I'll be sure to put on my best rags."

His fist tightened around the shoulder of the shirt he held in his hand, pressing wrinkles into the freshly ironed fabric. "You're lucky I even let you live after the disgrace you brought to this pack, Sarah."

"I'm not sure I'd call this living, *Dad*." Sarah flipped her hand around her to indicate the dusty basement, including the shabby bathroom with a leaky faucet and the makeshift bedroom she and Ava shared in the back corner.

"I am your Alpha!" Edward roared, taking a step forward. Spittle flew from his mouth and smacked onto the unfinished concrete floor. "You and your brat have been an embarrassment to this pack for years. Learn to obey me, or else." He gritted his teeth, shaking one angry hand toward Ava.

Sarah's heart clenched, but it was a different type of fear that shook her this time. She straightened her shoulders and lifted her chin as she stepped slightly to the side, putting herself between her father and daughter. There was little she could do if he decided to lose his temper, especially with this damn silver collar lying so heavily around her neck, but that wouldn't stop her from trying. She'd already done wrong by Ava in so many ways, but she couldn't let things go any further. "I'm sorry, Father." Her eyes held his steadily.

"As you should be." Still clutching his precious damn shirt, he turned and stormed back up the stairs. "Janice, where the hell is my cell phone? I can't find it anywhere."

When the door slammed behind him, a tiny giggle had Sarah turning toward her daughter in shock. "What's so funny?"

Ava's eyes were wide and glistening, and her lips were pressed together as she tried to hold back her laughter. She glanced at the ceiling and shrugged innocently.

Sarah would've thought Ava would be terrified after that encounter with her so-called grandfather, but that didn't seem to be the case. "Do you know where his phone is?"

Casually opening the dryer and pulling out a

clean towel, Ava began folding it on top of the washing machine. "How should I know where his phone is? It's not my responsibility to keep track of it. He might be surprised to find it under the bathroom sink, though. He really ought to be more careful."

Despite the desperation surrounding their situation, Sarah burst out laughing as she turned back to her ironing. "You little sneak! I have to admire your efforts, though. I'm just concerned that you'll get into more trouble than we can handle if you get caught."

Ava lifted her chin in a way that reminded Sarah too much of herself. "I'm not going to get caught."

"You don't know that," Sarah said quietly, wishing there was some way she could've protected Ava from this life.

More movement could be heard over their heads, something they were used to at this point. Sarah and Ava were only allowed in the rest of the packhouse when tasked with chores, returning to the basement as soon as they'd finished. They'd learned to recognize footsteps and determine where they were going. It definitely wasn't Edward this time; the steps were too light. Sarah's shoulders relaxed slightly.

Ava set another towel on the stack and reached back into the dryer. She stuck her nail under the silver collar around her neck and itched for a moment. "I'm careful, Mom. More careful than you can even imagine."

Sarah's heart twisted as her eyes rested on that horrid band of metal. She'd cried openly when a tiny collar had been clamped around Ava's neck when she was just a toddler, a punishment Sarah had thought her daughter wouldn't have to suffer along with her. They'd changed it out as she'd grown, but it never made Sarah feel any better about it. They both knew what it meant.

The collar was just the minimum punishment that could be inflicted on them if they didn't behave. Sarah could throw caution to the wind for her own sake, but not for her daughter's. "If you're up there causing trouble, then it's too much of a risk, Ava. I can't have anything happen to you."

Ava's eyes sparked once again. "I'll be fine, Mom. See, I—" She stopped, and her eyes flicked over to the stairs.

Sarah had been focusing on her too much to notice the quiet thump of the basement door. She turned to see her mother, carefully setting her feet down in just the right places to make as few creaks and squeaks as possible as she descended the staircase.

Janice glanced back up at the door when she reached the bottom of the steps, then hurried over to Sarah, holding out a single cupcake on a small plate. "Happy birthday, dear."

"Oh, Mom." Sarah took it in her hands as though it were made of gold. They weren't allowed niceties like this. A sugary treat might be an everyday occurrence for others, but not for her. She knew just how big of a risk her mother had taken by doing such a thing. "You didn't have to."

"Yes, I did." Janice looked like she was going to cry as she pulled a lighter and candle out of her pocket, even though she was trying her best to be brave. "Everyone deserves to have their birthday celebrated."

Holding the cupcake as her mother put the candle down through the frosting, Sarah felt tears burn the backs of her eyes. She'd tried not to think about it, but it was impossible. This was her son's birthday as well. How could she ever forget the day he came into the world and made her a mother for the first time? He'd changed her entire life, but Sarah knew she'd probably never get the chance to tell him so. At forty, she always thought she'd be driving her kids to soccer practice and looking at colleges with them. Instead, there she was, demoted to the lowest member of her pack, living a life of servitude with her daughter. "I've been trying not to think about it."

"I know, dear." Janice reached out to touch Sarah's hair, her sad eyes whisking over her face. She must not have liked what she saw because she soon returned her attention to the cupcake. "What are you going to wish for this year?"

Sarah closed her eyes. She remembered a time when she still believed in birthday wishes, when she'd sat at the dining table upstairs with the rest of the pack around her, trying to decide to wish for a pony or a kitten. There were times as a child when she'd resented the way the adults ran her life, when they wouldn't let her go where she wanted in the woods, or when she couldn't spend the night at a friend's house or participate in a pack run because she hadn't brought up her grades. Life had seemed so unfair, and she'd been bitter about the way she'd been imprisoned by rules and regulations.

Independence had come to mean something so much more than that.

Sarah didn't want a pony or a kitten. She

wouldn't wish for a new designer dress or a gorgeous car. There was only one thing she wanted as she opened her eyes and focused on the flame. Freedom.

With a long, slow breath, she blew out the candle.

2

THE WIND WHISTLED PAST MAX'S EARS AND RIPPLED through his fur. The day was too beautiful to waste, and he lifted his muzzle to inhale as much of it as he possibly could. After all, his son was only going to turn eighteen once. *You sure this is the only thing you wanted to do today?* Max asked through their telepathic link.

I didn't say it was the only *thing,* Hunter reminded him. *It's a great start, though.*

Brody pulled alongside them, easily flying through the woods on all fours. *I can't argue with that. There's nothing more freeing than this.*

Even so, we might want to turn and head back toward the packhouse. We've been out for a long time.

Not that Max would've minded spending the rest of the day like this. He'd gladly stop thinking about his job at the rock club, Selene's, and his duties as the Glenwood pack beta, just allowing himself to be a wolf for a while. He was forty-four now, but remembered what it was like to be young, and he wanted Hunter to enjoy it while he still could. But Max's mother, Joan, had planned plenty of festivities for the day, and he knew she'd never forgive him if they skipped out.

Fine, Hunter relented. *Let's at least go up here first.*

Max and Brody followed him up a steep and rocky path. Considering the trees in the way, it was barely a path at all, but wolves didn't need nicely groomed trails. Max bounded from one rock to another after his son, feeling a little of that youth himself, until they emerged into the sun of the ridgetop.

This is one of my favorite spots, Hunter admitted as he moved almost all the way to the edge and then sat on his haunches. *You can see it all from here.*

Stepping up on his left, Max had to agree with Hunter's assessment. They could see a vast amount of the Glenwood pack's territory, save what was naturally hidden by the trees. He knew they were fortunate to have so many wild acres to run on without much interference. Any hikers who came through there were probably lost, and seeing a pack of wolves running by would ensure they never returned. He thought of the packs who lived more modern lives, settling down in big cities and keeping their wolf forms at bay most of the time. Every pack was a bit different, but he was grateful to be a part of this one.

Brody came around on Hunter's right. *So, what are you thinking? You're eighteen now. You've got the rest of your adult life ahead of you. What are your plans?*

Oh, come on. I don't have to decide all of that right now, Hunter hedged.

Of course not, but you should at least pick a direction that you want to try out. You'll be graduating soon. Are you going to college?

Max gazed out over the treetops and let his mind wander while Hunter explained his plans to his uncle. He and Hunter had already had this conversation, and more than once. His son had been rather stubborn about it at first, insisting that school was a waste of time and there was nothing he was interested in pursuing as a career.

Somewhere along the line during his senior year,

that had changed. He wanted to go to college but stay local so he could still be close to the pack. Eugene University was at the top of his list, and Max had no doubt that was thanks to Conner. Hunter's cousin had come into the pack only recently, but the two young wolves had bonded quickly. While Conner was able to pursue his degree on a football scholarship, Hunter would be paying his own way. He was still exploring a few different programs, but he was leaning toward environmental studies. Max wouldn't be surprised if the kid stuck with it. He loved the land he'd grown up on.

Brody jostled Hunter's shoulder with his own. *If you ever decide you want to become a tattoo artist, just let me know. We could use more stand-up guys like you in the industry.*

I can't see anyone paying me to draw stick figures on them, Hunter retorted.

Hey, you never know what someone might want. You could specialize in shitty handwriting and awkward stick figures. You'd be the talk of the town. You just couldn't let anyone know that we're related. I have a business to uphold, you know.

Max loved seeing how close Hunter was with the rest of the pack. Most kids that age didn't want to be around their families, especially adults. Hunter was really starting to mature, though, and it showed. He didn't want to ruin their good time, but he knew he had to be the dad right now. *We'd really better get going.*

Fine. Hunter turned away from the ridge and slipped back down into the woods. *Hey, Brody. Since I'm eighteen now, I guess that means I can finally get a tattoo from you, right?*

Sure does. Brody was on Hunter's heels, keeping up just fine with the young wolf. *Have you been thinking about what you're going to get?*

Everything was changing for Hunter with this birthday. He could make bigger decisions for himself, like getting a tattoo. He was thinking about his future. He had the whole world in front of him.

Max knew he should be happier about it all, but this day was always a bit bittersweet for him. He hung back a little behind the others as he thought about Sarah. It'd been so long since he'd seen her, but her face hadn't faded in his mind. She had the most beautiful brown eyes, deep and bright, full of light and energy. Her dark blonde hair would shine in the sun, and those killer curves were everything he'd ever wanted back in his twenties. She'd been so excited the day she'd delivered their son. Not only had she finally met the baby she'd been growing for those long months, but they'd also be sharing the same birthday for the rest of their lives.

They'd never gotten to share any more after that first one.

Guilt rested like a heavy burden on Max's shoulders. It weighed him down on a continuous basis, but it was even worse on a day like today. How could he possibly think about Hunter and the day he came into this world without thinking about Sarah? How could he glance at his son, seeing her features reflected in his handsome young face, and not feel the pain of missing her all over again?

It was all his fault. As they reached the bottom of the steep slope and turned back toward a wider path, Max knew he'd never be able to convince himself otherwise. His parents had both tried, reminding him that the Alpha of the Greystone pack was known for being brutal and ruling with an iron fist. Max couldn't have done anything to change the outcome, they insisted. But Max knew better. If only he'd slowed down and listened. If only he'd reasoned with her. If only he'd suggested they take their time and come up with the right decisions together. He could wish all he wanted, but it wouldn't change a thing. She'd been killed, and he'd never seen her again.

The ground leveled out beneath them. Hunter kicked it into high gear, churning up dirt and grass under his paws as he streaked through the forest, and Brody was hot on his tail. After going for so long without finding his mate, Brody had finally found her in Robin. The two were the perfect match, a pair of souls that'd been undoubtedly bonded before either of them had reached this earth.

Someday, Hunter would be lucky enough to find his one true mate as well. It could hit him at any time, coming at him from out of nowhere and turning his wolf into a wild beast. He'd probably freak out a little if it happened while he was young. It was a feeling like nothing else, but Hunter would have his pack around him to help him get through it. Max looked forward to being part of his support system as he found his place in the world.

He slowed as they reached the clearing behind the packhouse. This was the last place he'd seen Sarah, the last place he'd ever feel the draw of a fated mate again. It pulled at him occasionally, tugging on his soul, but he knew his wolf was just holding out hope. It'd be easier if it left him alone. Instead, those little pangs of longing from his inner beast would keep him reaching out with his mind every now and then while in his wolf form. Just in case. Nothing. He would never know his fated love again.

"There he is!" Joan said as she came out the back door carrying a big platter toward a table already groaning with food.

Hunter easily morphed back into his human form without a hitch in his stride and slowed to a walk. "What's all this?"

"You didn't think I was just going to let your birthday go by unnoticed, did you?" Joan wrapped her grandson in a tight hug before she stepped back and held him at arm's length. "By Selene's blessing, you certainly have grown into a handsome young man."

"Oh, come on, Grandma." Hunter slouched to the side, trying to avoid her affections.

"*You* come on!" Joan insisted with a laugh as she mushed his cheeks between her hands. "I can't believe how lucky I am to have you."

"You're embarrassing me." His entire face was turning red.

"Why should you be embarrassed?" Brody asked as he reached into a cooler for a can of soda. "I mean, it's just us. And Lilah Fulton."

"What?" Hunter swiveled his head one way and then another, trying to find her.

Brody bent over at the waist, smacking his hand against his knee. "You're way too easy, man! It's just the pack right now. We figured whatever else you were doing with your friends would be happening later tonight."

"Who is this Lilah Fulton?" Dawn asked as she stepped out the back door with a bowl of potato salad. "Is she someone special? Do I need to meet her? Because you know Auntie Dawn is here to protect you from all those fierce females."

"Thanks, but no thanks." Finally released from his grandmother's grasp, Hunter sat down at one of the tables right across from his uncle, Rex. "Save me from these women!"

"As if I'd even dare." The Alpha of the Glenwood pack grabbed a chicken leg and put it on his plate. "Now that you're old enough, I think it's time I let you in on a little secret. The men are never the ones in charge, Hunter. It's the women. It's always the women."

"That's not true," Lori said as she sat down beside her mate. The pack Luna tipped her head to the side as she buttered an ear of corn, smiling. "Well, maybe it is."

"Sure, it is," Brody agreed. He'd just taken his baby daughter Evelyn from Robin's arms. "I mean, I know this little lady is definitely in charge of our lives."

Max joined the group, hardly realizing exactly when he'd changed back into his human form. He was close to his pack, but today he felt the distance between himself and the rest of the Glenwoods. It was as though he was watching it all on a TV show, some happy, friendly sitcom where everyone teased each other gently but ultimately had each other's backs. He focused on the smokey aroma of the chicken legs and tried to ground himself back in reality, but things would never just be normal, no matter how hard he pretended.

Hunter had grown up without his mother, and Max knew the strong women of the Glenwood pack were responsible for him turning out as well-balanced as he had. Ironically, those same strong women were the reason the Greystones had forbidden Sarah and Max's relationship.

Max wasn't hungry, but he forced himself to eat. He felt Dawn's eyes on him, and she quirked a brow at him when he looked over. Max gave the slightest shake of his head. She knew how rough today would be for him, but he didn't need her to make a big deal out of it. What was done was done. There was nothing he could do to fix it. Finding another woman to be with, someone who could warm his bed at night and act as a mom to Hunter, wasn't in the cards for him. He wouldn't settle. As the rest of the pack gathered around them, joining in the celebration of Hunter's big day, Max had to hope they'd be enough for him.

3

"Mom."

"Hm?" Sarah tasted the tuna salad, noting it needed more lemon juice.

"I have a birthday present for you," Ava whispered.

Sarah nearly dropped the large wooden spoon she'd been stirring with. She whipped her head around to make sure no one else was within earshot in the expansive kitchen. Edward never left them completely unguarded, especially when he wasn't going to be home. He'd taken all the top members of the pack out to his favorite steakhouse that night, which was why he'd wanted that blue shirt. Sarah knew he'd only gone out to rub her faults in her face once again. It was *her* birthday, and *she* should be the one out at a restaurant with her pack around her. Edward would take every chance he could to make sure she knew just how much shame she'd brought him.

They were relatively safe for the moment, at least. The guards Edward put in place wouldn't notice anything as long as Sarah was doing what she was supposed to. "I don't need a birthday present, sweetheart. I don't want to risk anyone having any reason to punish us more than they already have." Or at least, she didn't want Ava to be punished. The poor girl was serving a prison sentence simply for existing, which was unfair enough.

"But up here is where it's the most fun to do it," Ava insisted, her brows knitting together as she bounced on her toes with urgency. "It won't be the same if I wait."

Sarah added more lemon juice to the tuna salad and gave it a stir. The huge bowl of it would feed most of the pack during the next meeting. Sarah and Ava would be lucky if they got any. She transferred it into a large container with a lid and then rinsed out the bowl, using the spray of the water to help cover her voice. "What on earth are you talking about?"

"Just let me show you. It's better that way. I'll be quick," Ava insisted.

Though she couldn't imagine what Ava was up to, Sarah could see how important this was to her daughter. The girl had so little else to look forward to, so how could she refuse? Sarah glanced at the kitchen doorway once again to make sure no one was coming. "All right."

"Okay. Look at that bottle of dish soap." Ava bit her lip in excitement.

She did as she was told. It was just a plain bottle of blue dish soap sitting next to the sink, awaiting the special coffee cups Edward loved, which all had to be washed by hand. "Okay."

"Keep your eye on it."

"I am," Sarah promised. What were normal teen girls having fun with these days? Playing on their cell phones and constantly snapping photos of themselves, from what Sarah understood. Dish soap wouldn't intrigue them.

Ava pulled in a deep breath and let it out slowly. She held out a finger, rolling it through the air and then flicking it to the right. The bottle of soap disappeared.

Sarah blinked. She slowly set the bowl she'd been rinsing down in the sink and took a step closer to the counter, sure that she'd missed something. Reaching a hand out, she touched the corner of the sink where the bottle had been only a moment ago. "What happened?"

"Look over there." Ava was practically giggling now.

She swerved her eyes to the right to find the bottle several feet away on the counter. A little bubble hovered near the top of it and popped.

Sarah's knees grew weak. She leaned against the counter as she studied her daughter. She'd seen Ava every single day of her life, and during those days, they spent hardly any time apart. This was absolutely unbelievable. "Did you just do what I think you did?"

Ava nodded her head vigorously. "Yeah! Isn't it amazing?"

"I..." Sarah searched for the right words. She was blown away and never expected anything like this. "Yes. But how? The most I've ever seen is when you made a little spark of light on the tip of your finger when you were afraid of the dark."

She'd been terrified for her daughter once she'd seen the evidence that Ava had inherited more from the Glenwood lineage than Max's bright blue eyes. If Edward or any of his accomplices found out, it would surely be the end of her.

That terror took over her once again, now that

they were talking about far more than just a spark of light. Quickly, Sarah hustled Ava into the pantry. "Did you really just use magic in there?"

"Yep! I've been working on it whenever you weren't looking. I wanted to wait to show you until I could do something special." Ava studied her fingertip. "I know it's just a bottle of soap, but let me know if you need to get anything from the top shelf."

Sarah clasped Ava's hands between her own. "No! Don't get me wrong, Ava. It's the most amazing thing I've ever seen. But if you get caught—"

"I haven't yet," her daughter insisted. Her enthusiasm had now turned into determination. "I've already done it a bunch of times, which is how I knew it would work this time."

"And that's how you've been able to hide Edward's cell phone or make him think he'd lost his keys again," Sarah realized. Ava's pranks had always made Sarah worry, but now she was even more concerned. This wasn't simple teenage rebellion. It was something much more, something that could possibly enrage Edward Greystone into doing something drastic.

Ava, however, was too happy with her accomplishment to be thinking of such things. "Do you remember when you used to tell me all those stories about witches and magic when I was little?"

"How could I forget?" Sweet little Ava, tucked up against Sarah's side in that musty basement. She'd been so small back then. Even her voice had been tiny, and Sarah loved nothing more than when the two of them could steal a few moments to snuggle up and talk. "You loved those stories."

"And that's what I thought they were," Ava continued. "I thought they were fairytales, just something from a book. I didn't realize until recently that they were true. There really are people who can harness magic, who can make the world change. I'm one of them, Mom. I can feel it inside me."

Her throat was tight. "What's different? I mean, what's different now instead of when you did the thing with the light?"

Ava lifted her hands in the air. "It's just a feeling about it. It's something inside me. I don't really know how to explain it."

Sarah bit her lip. She'd helped her daughter learn to walk. She'd taught her how to read and write. Then there had been her first period. Those challenges now sounded so simple compared to what she had before her now. "I wish I knew what to tell you, but the truth is that I don't know much of anything about it."

"You do, though." Ava pulled her hand out of her mother's grasp and rested her fingers on Sarah's upper arms. "You spent time with the people on Dad's side of the family. You told me that you'd seen them work their magic before. Again, at the time, I thought it was just a story. But you were there. You can tell me."

"Oh, honey." Sarah pressed her hand to her forehead. Yes, she'd seen some things. It wasn't the same as knowing, not when it came down to something like this. She might as well try to explain to a human what it was like to be a shifter. "Your grandmother and your Aunt Dawn, they're witches. Real-life ones, unlike the characters in those books we had when you were little."

"What can they do?" The light in Ava's eyes was so bright and powerful.

Sarah saw that excitement and enthusiasm, and it shot another streak of pain through her heart. Ava was a teenager. She *should* be feeling that way about things, yet Sarah knew this was a very dangerous thing for them. Would she really be doing Ava any favors if she tried to deny it all, though? "Let's see. I'm trying to remember, but it was a long time ago.

Dawn was studying to be a nurse, and I've seen her heal both with her hands and powers. Joan, your grandmother, could do all sorts of things. She could use it to fight, to move objects, to unlock doors. There's probably a lot more that I just don't recall." Sarah knew that she herself would never be able to do the things that Joan and Dawn did. Her family had no witch bloodline, but that was exactly the problem.

The tip of Ava's tongue darted out to the corner of her mouth for a moment. "Could she teleport things? Like what I did in the kitchen?"

"Yes. I saw her do that a few times. Sometimes it was just because the item she wanted was across the room." Sarah smiled at the memory. Joan was a powerful woman, the Luna of the Glenwood pack back then. She had the ultimate respect of her pack, but that didn't stop them from teasing her when she used her abilities so that she didn't have to get up and walk across the room to turn on the light.

"And could she teleport people?" Ava pressed.

"I don't know. I never saw her do it, anyway. I imagine that wouldn't be easy." Sarah paused, and her eyes drifted from the row of canned peaches on a nearby shelf up to her daughter's face. "Why?"

If she thought Ava had looked excited before, it

was nothing compared to the exhilaration she saw now. "See, that's why me moving that little soap bottle is my birthday present to you. I figured if I work on it a little more, I might be able to try it on us." She wiggled her finger back and forth in the air between the two of them.

"You mean..."

"Yes! I'd only have to do it once, and then we'd be outside. We could get away," Ava insisted.

Sarah gaped at her. Over the last several years, she'd paid attention to the behaviors and schedules of the guards. She'd glanced up at the cameras that looked over every exit to the house, wondering if she could do anything to turn them off. When Ava had been very small, Sarah had even imagined strapping her daughter to her chest and just running like hell. These mental experiments had always ended up with them getting caught, and the results weren't ones she liked to entertain. But this was a wholly different thing. If Ava's magic was strong enough, and if she could get them far enough away, then there was a chance.

"Hey! What are you doing in there?"

Sarah startled at the question and quickly grabbed a carton of chicken broth. "Just gathering everything we need to make some soup tomorrow."

Frank, the guard who'd been left in charge of them that evening, appeared in the pantry's doorway. He scowled at her, the look enhanced by the thin line of a scar that ran from his forehead to his jawline. "Hmph."

"What did you think we were doing in the pantry?" Sarah challenged as she pushed her way past him. "Digging our way out with a spoon?"

"I wouldn't put it past you," he grumbled. Frank stood back just enough to let them through, then shut the pantry door behind them. He continued to stand there, watching them with suspicion.

"Why, Frank, you give me far too much credit. Keep that up, and I just might start to think you like me."

His suspicion turned to disgust, and he stalked back into the living room.

Letting out a breath, Sarah pulled a large pot out of a lower cabinet and set it on the stove. She hadn't actually planned to make soup, but she figured she ought to now. Frank wasn't exactly a genius, but the last thing she needed was for him to think she and Ava had been discussing something that would piss Edward off.

Apparently, she'd trained Ava well in this regard. The girl had grabbed the bag of onions from the pantry and set two of them out on a cutting board. "Figured you'd want these," she said glumly.

"Yes, thank you. Probably some celery and carrots, too. Chicken and rice sounds good to me." Sarah went through the motions, knowing that having something to occupy their time up there would keep them from having to go straight back down to the basement. It wasn't much freedom, but she'd take any sliver she could get.

Pain ensconced her heart as she replayed the conversation they'd just had in the pantry. Ava was delighted with what she'd been able to teach herself to do, and she truly believed she could use that talent to rescue them. It was a clever idea, but it also drove home just how much this lifestyle of theirs was her own fault.

The onion and celery went in the bottom of the pot with a pat of butter, sizzling away and filling the kitchen with their earthy fragrance. Sarah added minced garlic and poked it around in the bottom of the pan. Some memories had become fuzzy over time, but one was just as clear as if it'd happened yesterday. Sarah had stormed out of the Glenwood packhouse, so pissed, she could be steaming. She'd just planned to go for a walk. Max was still at home with their son, but if she didn't leave for a bit to clear her head, she was going to say something she might regret.

She never expected to be captured right there on Glenwood territory.

When Edward's guards had locked her in the basement of the Greystone packhouse, she'd spent hours pounding on that door. The dents and scratch marks her rage had created could still be seen there. "Let me out of here, you assholes! Max is going to come over here and beat you to a bloody pulp!"

She'd been so worked up that she hadn't even pulled back when Edward had yanked open the door, his face red and twisted as he snarled at her. "He won't, Sarah, and do you want to know why? I went right up and told him to his face that you were dead, which is what should've happened, anyway."

"He won't believe you," she'd insisted, already feeling the hope dying inside her. "He'll know better. You wouldn't kill me."

"Wouldn't I?" Edward had slammed the door in her face and slid a heavy bolt into place.

Slumping down, Sarah had sat on that top step for hours. Tears had slid down her cheeks and soaked her shirt, but a numbness overcame her. Max wouldn't be coming. Anyone might believe that Edward had eliminated her so he wouldn't have to deal with her anymore. There was no reason for Max not to believe him.

For those first several months, Sarah had beat herself up inside for what she'd done. She'd acted like an idiot, running away from her problems with Max instead of facing them head-on. It was her fault that she was in this situation, and there would be no getting out of it.

Pulling herself back out of the dreamlike state the memory had left her in, Sarah looked at Ava. She was a beautiful young thing, almost as tall as Sarah was now. Sarah hadn't even known she was pregnant with her when she'd been captured. The news had both devastated her and given her a spark of hope. Ava had brought life back to Sarah, and now it was time for Sarah to do the same thing for her. "Can you come help me get the last ingredients out of the pantry?"

"Sure." Ava put down the knife she was using to slice the carrots and followed her.

Sarah plucked a bag of rice from the shelf and handed it to her. She rested her hands on it even as Ava took it, meeting her eyes. "Do it, honey. If you think you can, then do it."

Ava beamed. "Okay, Mom. Let's get out of here."

4

"Janice!"

Sarah cringed as she heard her father bellow for her mother. It was nothing unusual. Even if he was in the same room, Edward had a way of commanding all the attention. He spoke louder and walked heavier than was necessary. He bragged about every tiny thing he could think of, throwing around prestige as though he'd done something magnificent to become the Alpha of the Greystones instead of simply inheriting the title. Sarah went back to scrubbing the bathtub.

"Janice!" Edward repeated, his voice reverberating throughout the hallway at Sarah's back. "What time is the thing tonight?"

Sarah slowed her scrubbing. Her fingernail still forced a corner of the sponge in between the tile grout, but she was no longer paying attention to the job she'd been assigned. What thing? If something was going on in the packhouse, she needed to know about it.

"Eight," came Janice's softer voice from a little further away. "We need to make sure we leave by seven-thirty to get there on time."

"Is there no end to all the things an Alpha has to do?" Edward grumbled. "I'm busy enough as it is, but now I have to go to some ridiculous party. Won't I get a break from all this hard work at some point?"

Sarah smirked. Hard work, her ass. The only hard work he did was making sure Sarah and Ava's lives were as miserable as possible.

"I'm sure you will, dear," Sarah's mother reassured him. "And we only have to stay for a couple of hours. Molly and Ryan are so excited about their new place and are throwing a housewarming party to share it with everyone. They've been planning it forever. And, of course, there's no way they would've been able to get such a lovely home if you hadn't given them the start they'd needed here with the rest of the pack."

"That's true. I guess I ought to at least enjoy some of the fruits of my labor and get a free meal. What am I supposed to wear?"

Their voices receded down the hallway, and Sarah could no longer hear what they were saying. She fervently resumed cleaning the tub, wiping down the walls and hosing out the corners with the shower head. She gave the shampoo and soap bottles a cursory wipe before she chucked them back on the shelves, not paying much attention to where they went. It was only four o'clock. That meant they had a few hours yet before Edward was out of the house.

Good on Janice for cajoling Edward, playing into his ego to get him to stop whining. Had she done that on purpose, knowing that Sarah might hear her? Probably not. Janice sympathized with her, and she showed Sarah kindness whenever she had the chance, but she feared her husband more than anything else. She also knew that Edward had wired the whole place up with that security system of his and that even if Sarah and Ava had been left completely alone, they'd never get past the threshold without someone knowing about it.

The sink and toilet were already done. All that

was left was to grab the bag from the trash can under the sink. Sarah grinned as she did so, wishing she could've been there when Edward found his cell phone in just that spot. The man was known for throwing fits, and if he had any idea what his grand-daughter was capable of doing, he would've blown a gasket.

It was hard to force herself to walk slowly through the house with the trash bag in one hand and her rubber gloves in the other. Sarah casually moseyed to the garage door, opened it, and chucked the bag into the bin that would go to the curb the following day. Several other Greystones were milling around, ignoring her as they'd been told to. She slipped back down into the basement, her heart thundering and her mind whirring, hoping no one could tell.

"Ava!"

"Geez, you scared the crap out of me!" Ava jumped back from the utility sink. "I guess I got a little too involved in what I was doing."

"What *are* you doing?" Sarah had left Ava to take care of the laundry since she'd have some privacy down there in the basement. The washer and dryer were running, but Ava was standing at the sink.

"Washing this little guy. Isn't he cute?" Ava

stepped back just enough to show her mother the small dog sitting placidly in the sink, lounging in a few inches of soapy water.

"A dog? Where did he come from?" Sarah held out her hand and let the little terrier mix sniff it. One of his ears stood straight up, and the other flopped forward. He blinked his warm brown eyes as he sniffed her hand, then ducked his muzzle under her fingers.

"Gina, of all people," Ava snorted. "She came down here and pretty much shoved him at me. I guess she adopted him from a shelter. She said she didn't want to see him again until he literally smelled like roses, and there wasn't even the ghost of a flea on him."

"Oh, boy. I feel sorry for the poor thing if he belongs to Gina now." Sarah scratched around behind his ears. Her Aunt Gina had never been a pleasant person, even before Sarah was in her current predicament. She believed she held a special status by being the Alpha's sister, though she—like Edward—didn't do anything to deserve it. Gina treated just about everyone like peasants, which had always gotten under Sarah's skin. She was the last person Sarah would've expected to own a dog.

Ava drained the sink. She turned on the faucet,

holding the stream of water out of the way while she checked the temperature with her free hand before giving the dog a rinse. "I don't think she's even given him a name yet, or at least she didn't tell me. He's a sweet thing, though, and he didn't seem to mind the bath at all. He even let me wash his belly. Didn't you, handsome man? Didn't you?" Ava pursed her lips into a kissy face and was rewarded with a swipe of the dog's tongue across her chin.

"I'm sorry you had to deal with her." Sarah had been stunned to find the dog, but there was much more important news she needed to share. "Edward and Janice are going to a housewarming party tonight. They're leaving at seven-thirty, and they'll be gone for at least a couple of hours."

With one hand still on the dog to make sure he didn't leap out of the sink, Ava looked up at the floor joists above them. "Do you think everyone is going?"

"I don't know," Sarah admitted. "I think it's a good possibility. It's for a young couple in the pack who just bought a house, and Janice said they wanted to share their new place with everyone. It could be our chance."

Ava grabbed a nearby towel and began drying the dog. "I haven't heard Edward or anyone else yell at you for a while, so maybe they don't think they need to leave too many people here."

"We can hope." Sarah had made several escape attempts during the first couple of years of her captivity. She'd been caught every time, but it hadn't stopped her from trying something else. She hadn't tried in ages, and even though Edward hated her guts, he didn't seem particularly concerned that she might actually get away. Not after all this time. "What do you think?"

The question twisted her gut as she asked it. Sarah hated to put this kind of pressure on her daughter, even if it was Ava's idea. They'd be relying almost solely on her magic to get away, and it was an unfair burden for a child.

Fortunately, Ava didn't seem bothered by it in the least. Instead, she gave her mother one of her classic grins. "I think I have something to show you."

"Things are...progressing?" Sarah asked. It was such a hard balance to show Ava that she had confidence in her while not trying to sound too hopeful or desperate. Being a mother was challenging enough, even more so in these circumstances.

"You tell me." Ava turned back to the sink. Just as she'd done in the kitchen, she swirled her finger in the air and then flicked it to the side.

Sarah's stomach sunk back toward her spine as the terrier disappeared from the sink. He was now on the floor, standing between the two of them. "Is he all right?" Her voice was barely a whisper.

"It doesn't seem to bother him any more than the bath does." Using the towel, Ava scooped up the dog and held him in her arms. "What do you think? Are you okay? Is your tum-tum upset or anything?"

The dog wagged his tail and panted happily.

Sarah realized she was holding her hand to her chest and quickly dropped it. "I guess you really have been practicing."

"The soap was easy, so I just started working on bigger and bigger things. When I managed to rearrange the whole bedroom and put it back together again, I knew I needed to go somewhere from there. I need to do it with something living, you know? So when I was upstairs a few days ago, I moved that potted plant by the front window. It didn't do so much as drop a leaf, so I figured this was the next best step."

It was all perfectly reasonable, and there was no doubt that Ava was talented. She had to be to teach herself something like this. Adrenaline coursed through Sarah's veins. "I guess that means we know what we're doing tonight."

———————

SARAH HAD ALWAYS HATED BEING USED AS A household servant, but that night, she was using it to her advantage. She picked up the desk chair in the guest bedroom and hauled it down the hallway to set it in the living room.

Frank was lounging on the couch, flicking through videos on the huge television. He glanced over his shoulder at her. "How long are you going to have all that crap out here?"

It wasn't all that much, really: the chair, some totes from under the bed, a small side table that could be easily moved, and a floor lamp. The massive living room had plenty of space for it. "Well, it's going to take at least an hour to clean the carpet, and then it has to dry before I can put any of this back. It might be tonight, or it might be tomorrow."

"If it's tonight, then you damn well better get it out of the living room before Edward gets home. I don't want to hear it when he comes in and trips over something." Frank clamped his finger down on the remote and flicked to a different video.

"That's a good idea. Thank you." Sarah repressed the urge to make some sarcastic remark about Frank being the only thing someone would trip over because he was nothing more than a useless waste of space, but she didn't need to call any extra attention to herself.

Ava came through the kitchen doorway with the carpet shampooer she'd just fetched from the garage.

"Is that thing going to be loud? I'm trying to watch something here." He used the remote to gesture toward the TV as though it were the most important thing in the world.

Sarah made a face. "Yeah, it's kind of loud. But I'll shut the door so it won't be too bad."

"Fine." He turned his back toward her.

Ava stuck her tongue out at him and then headed down the hall.

Sarah followed and shut the door firmly behind them. "Let's get that thing started up as quickly as possible."

"I've got it all filled up." Ava plugged the machine in.

Sarah took it from her. She pulled the handle back and flicked the switch. The shampooer roared to life, louder even than the vacuum. A squeeze of the trigger sent soapy water out onto the carpet, and Sarah began working near the door, gliding the machine back and forth in slow strokes. She realized her hands were shaking. No, her entire body was shaking. Their entire future rested on this plan. Doubts had been swimming in her head all afternoon. What if too many people had stayed behind at the packhouse? Even after she'd gotten permission to clean the carpets, she worried about whether or not someone would catch on to what they were doing. In a way, the plan couldn't be any better. They had all the cover they needed, and if they pulled this off, no one would know they were gone for quite some time. If they didn't, well, she didn't want to think about that.

Ava tapped her shoulder and nodded. That was the signal they'd agreed on. Leaving the shampooer running, Sarah clicked the handle back into place. Frank could likely hear the faint noise of it from where he was sitting, and he'd assume they were right where they were supposed to be. Sarah came and stood next to her daughter.

She felt Ava pull in a deep breath. Her finger didn't merely make a small circle in the air this time, considering the subject of her spell was much larger. She made a fluid motion with her arm and then flicked it away.

Complete blackness took over Sarah's vision. Her lungs wouldn't work, and every part of her body tingled with electric energy. Then she was struggling to keep her feet underneath her. The floor was tipping, and she couldn't get her balance. No, not the floor. The *roof.*

"Mom!" Ava reeled backward, her arms flinging out wildly on either side of her.

Instinctively, Sarah grabbed her wrist and pulled her close as she thrust herself toward the slope of the roof. The soles of her shoes caught on the roughness of the shingles. They lay there for a long moment, bracing themselves against the roof, catching their breath.

"Shit." Sarah's voice was breathy and nervous. Her heart pounded in her ears, and she felt like she was in some sort of crazy dream. "Are you okay?"

"Yeah." Ava lifted her head enough to look around, and when she looked past her feet and saw the ground, she quickly closed her eyes and buried her face in her mom's shoulder. "That's not what I meant to do."

"It's okay, baby." Sarah wrapped her arm around her, hating the terror in her daughter's voice. "It's okay. We made it. We're all right. We just have to get down to the ground. It's too steep right here, but we need to get someplace where the drop isn't too much." Of all the things she tried to think about ahead of time, ending up on the roof wasn't one of them.

"Oh, god." Ava swallowed and clung to her tightly.

Sarah felt that sentiment down to her very soul. If they went crawling across the roof, Frank might hear them. They'd have to not only survive the drop to the ground, but come out uninjured so they'd still be able to haul their asses out of there. There was no going back, though. They'd have to find a way to get through it. "Ava, honey. I want you to look at something. Don't look down at your feet; just look where I'm pointing."

Slowly, Ava lifted her head. Her eyes traced a line from Sarah's shoulder, down her arm, and across the property toward the woods. "What am I looking at?"

"That tree line over there. That's where we need to go once we get down on the ground." It'd been an eternity since she'd seen it, and even though some of the branches had become overgrown over the years, she knew it well.

"Okay, but how are we going to get down?" Ava clung to her the same way she had when she was little, her fingers clutching Sarah, not able to get close enough.

"I know it's a lot, but do you think you can use your magic again? If you can get us down onto the ground and in that direction, then we can go. We can just go. You don't even have to get us all the way there." Freedom was so close she could taste it, and the coppery bite of fear was right behind it. "We have to do something, and I think that's the best place to start. Can you do it?"

Ava's sweet brown eyes looked into hers, and it was impossible not to see her as a little girl. Her breath was coming fast and she was shaking all over, but she swallowed and nodded. "I'll try."

"That's my girl. Just remember, you do what you can, and I promise it'll be good enough." Sarah held tight to her daughter.

Ava's finger trembled when she began her circle. She clamped it back down, took a deep breath, then started again, slightly more steady this time. She circled and flung, making sure to point straight out into the field toward the tree line.

That same black, suffocating darkness came over Sarah for a split second before the earth came up and whacked her in the back. Any air she had left in her lungs escaped all at once. She gasped, trying to breathe. Fear rippled through her as tall grass swayed gently on either side of them.

"We made it," she managed to croak. "You did it, honey. We made it."

Tears rolled down from Ava's eyes toward her ears as she looked up at the sky. "I don't ever want to do that again."

"Hopefully, you won't need to." Sarah pressed a kiss to her forehead.

"I don't even think I can. I'm so tired." Ava rubbed her vibrating hands over her face. "I always got a little tired when I was doing the spells on other objects, but this is harder."

"I know, honey, but we're not done yet." Sarah listened, waiting for shouts or pounding footsteps. Could anyone from the packhouse see them out there in the field? Had Frank come to check on them yet and found only the shampooer running on its own? "We've got to get up, and we've got to run. It's going to be hard, but we can't give up now."

Ava nodded as she slowly sat up. "Okay."

Sarah peeked over the tall grass. It was getting dark now, but she could easily spot that special place in the trees. She just had to hope it was open enough for them to slip through. "Are you ready? Because we have to go as soon as we're on our feet. No dilly-dallying."

"I always hated when you said that." Ava smiled and shook her head while she took stock of her body. "Okay. I can do it."

"Good girl. Come on." Sarah reached out for Ava's hand. They launched to their feet and ran. Fear carried her forward at first, and she was certain that someone would attack, someone she hadn't antici-pated. That was what had happened before. Her love for her daughter made her feet fly through the field. She wasn't as strong as she used to be. Even with all the chores she did, it wasn't the same as running. Her muscles quickly fatigued and started to burn, but she pushed them on until they reached the trees.

Sarah ducked through first, throwing herself under a low-hanging branch. Thorns caught on her jeans and tugged, pulling her back toward the terrible life she was trying so hard to escape, but she pushed past them. No damn pricker bush was going to get in the way now. The path was so narrow that it was hardly even a path at all, and she hoped she still knew the way.

"Where are we going to go?" Ava asked.

That was the one part of this scheme that Sarah hadn't revealed to Ava. It wouldn't be easy on either of them, and there was no guarantee that it would work. She had hope, but what if they turned her away? It'd been so long, and she had no doubt that she'd caused them grief. "A place where I think we can find help. We've just got to get there as fast as we can."

5

"That was awesome! Did you see the way I took Conner out?" Hunter asked as he came through the back door with a grin, tossing his dark hair out of his eyes.

"Yup," Brody replied. He reached over and ruffled Hunter's hair, making him duck away and smooth it down.

"*Everyone* saw," Conner added. "And you're never going to let me live it down, are you?"

Hunter lifted his shoulders. "Guess we'll just have to see what happens next week."

"You're on!" Conner poked a finger into Hunter's chest before he headed for the fridge.

"Good training session?" Max asked from his

spot at the kitchen table. Pride swelled in his chest, which was happening an awful lot lately.

"Hell, yeah! Brody bores the hell out of me when it's all about footwork and repeating moves, but this time we got to spar." Hunter darted around Conner's position at the fridge and grabbed a cold bottle of water.

"It's all about muscle memory," Brody reminded the younger wolf casually. "It might sound boring right now, but it could really help you in the future. We've discussed this."

Hunter wasn't interested in any of that. His face was alight with his victory. "Anyway, Brody doesn't always let me go against Conner anymore. He says it doesn't do the pack any good to just have to top two going head to head all the time."

"Are you just going to keep talking about me like I'm not here?" Brody asked dramatically. "And after all I've done for you."

A slight smile crept over Max's face, even though he'd felt nothing but gloomy all day. He had this deep, unsettling feeling as though there was something he ought to be doing but wasn't. His wolf was restless, making it impossible to focus. He grounded himself in his son's training, hoping it would help. "Brody's right, you know. It's great if you and Conner are always at the top of the class, but that means the other wolves could really benefit from sparring with you. They'll learn things that they never would if they were only paired up with others on the same level. It's the same reason you boys have to fight me or Brody sometimes."

"Yeah, yeah. I know. But this was way more fun." Hunter slid into a chair across the table from his father. "We were up in the clearing, and the two of us had been going at it for a while, popping in and tagging each other here and there. You know how Brody will step in every minute or so and stop things, pointing out what should've gone differently?"

Max nodded. It amused him that Hunter wanted to speak as though Max had never been involved in these sessions himself, but he wasn't going to correct him. This was just his son's enthusiasm bubbling over. Fighting was a skill Hunter would need at some point. As the sole Glenwood heir at the moment, there was a chance he could become Alpha some-day, and Max didn't want to deter him in any way.

"Well, he wasn't doing that this time. He just put the two of us together in the clearing and let us go. I was a little thrown off at first because I kept waiting for him to say something," Hunter continued.

"Someone won't always be there to act as referee," Brody noted. He was leaning against the breakfast bar, looking proud.

"When I realized it, I started to get really excited. It got to me, and I slipped up and gave Conner a chance to pin me."

Conner put a platter of cold cuts on the counter and pulled off the cover. "You don't have to slip up for me to pin you."

"So he had me down, right?" Hunter slammed his hand on the kitchen table. "I was on the ground with half my face in the dirt. Conner is on top of me, and he's heavy even when he's in wolf form. He was just about to get my throat, and I thought that was it. In another second, I just knew Brody was going to call it. I couldn't stand the thought, though. I knew there had to be something I could do. My front legs were pretty much bound up, but I used my back legs to take his hind end down."

"And then I fell on my ass, and he pinned me instead," Conner concluded for him. "Brody, please tell me we can get back out there sooner than later so I don't have to keep hearing his victory speech."

"Oh, we will," Hunter promised, "but only so I can kick your ass again. You should've been there, Dad. It was amazing."

Guilt stabbed at his heart all over again. Hunter had Max's dark hair, but it was impossible not to see Sarah in his face. It was more pronounced when he was excited like this. He'd already denied his son a mother. Was he now being a bad father because he hadn't gone to the training session? And all because he was feeling moody? Shit. He just couldn't win for losing. "I'll be there next time."

Conner came around the breakfast bar. "How about we try this again right now? I just downloaded the latest edition of CyberBattle Apocalypse."

Hunter leaped up from his place at the table. "You're on!"

Snagging the plate of meat, the two boys thundered down to the basement.

Brody laughed. "I guess they can go kick each other's asses in a video game now. They ought to be exhausted. I know I am. I'm heading home."

"I'll see you." Max knew he should be getting home himself. He had the opening shift at Selene's the next day, and he didn't like just rolling out of bed and driving to work. Standing up and stretching, he padded toward the basement to tell Hunter he'd see him back at home.

A knock at the front door stopped him.

"Who the fuck could this be?" He wasn't in the

mood for visitors, and as far as he knew, they weren't expecting anyone. The rest of the packhouse had mostly disappeared for the evening, so Max stomped to the door and yanked it open.

His wolf immediately slammed against the underside of his skin. His foul mood collided with shock, wonder, and something else he knew couldn't be right. The two creatures that composed Max twisted and bent as he stared at the woman on the front porch.

She looked like his Sarah. She had that same dark blonde hair, though the light picked out a few strands of gray. There were those same brown eyes, the ones that had haunted his sleep and pulled at his heart every time he looked at his son. Tiny lines framed their corners.

It couldn't be her. She'd been dead for sixteen years. He'd never forget the day she'd gone missing, nor the announcement from Edward Greystone that he'd culled his own pack to defend his honor. The human side of Max tried to find the logic in this situation, to meld what he knew to be true with what he was seeing right in front of him. He'd been thinking about Sarah a lot over the past week or so. She'd been constantly at the forefront of his mind ever since Hunter's birthday, and it was making his eyes play tricks on him.

His wolf had other ideas. It was going wild, thrashing around inside him and snapping its jaws as it insisted that even the few feet between them were too much. It knew. She wasn't the same as when she'd left him; she was older now. Her face and body had changed, but it was absolutely her.

"Sarah. I..." His voice was strangled as he tried to force her name past his lips. "I thought you were dead."

"I know." Tears welled in her eyes, and she blinked them away quickly. "I know you did, and I'm sorry to just show up like this. I wouldn't do this to you if I had any other choice." Sarah glanced over her shoulder into the darkness that now cloaked the front yard.

The panic in her voice only escalated his wolf's agitation. Something was wrong, more than the fact his mate was alive when he'd thought otherwise for so long. Max stepped back and held the door wide. "It's all right. Just come in."

"Thank you, but I think I have to explain something first. There's someone here you need to meet. Someone who's wanted to meet you for a long time." Sarah looked over her shoulder again, but this time she wasn't looking off into the night for monsters. She stepped slightly to the side. "Come on, honey."

A teenager stepped into the yellow pool of the porch light. If Hunter was a mix of Max and Sarah, then this girl was an equal mix of them in the opposite way. Her hair was almost the exact same shade as Sarah's, dark and light blonde mixing in a natural blend of highlights. His own eyes stared at him, terrified, exhausted, expectant. The familiarity of her face stunned him, and he gripped the doorknob until his knuckles hurt. If she'd been dressed differently and turned her face just a little to the side, she'd look exactly like his mother in one of the old framed photos in the hallway.

"Max, this is your daughter, Ava." Sarah's chest heaved as her eyes flicked back and forth between the two of them. "I was pregnant when I walked out of the house that night, but I didn't know. My father had his men come after me, and they've been holding me ever since. I wanted so badly for you to know, but I couldn't. I couldn't get away, not until now."

There were so many questions swirling through Max's brain that he could hardly tell one from the other or know where to start. His wolf reminded him once again of the panic in Sarah's voice. He knew she wasn't scared of him. Something else was going on here. "Come in. Just come in."

Sarah stepped through the doorway with Ava on her heels. She stopped in the entryway, her hands knotted in front of her. "I'm really sorry about all of this, Max."

"No, it's..." He stared at them in turn. He was about to say it was all right, but it wasn't. He wasn't sure he'd ever be all right again. They'd been out there in the world all this time. His wolf had tried to tell him, nagging the back of his mind with those tugging feelings that he'd brushed off. Max's job as a mate and father was to protect those he loved. He didn't yet understand what had happened, but he knew he'd failed. His eyes traced down to the thick silver collars that lay heavily around their necks and drove the truth home.

His eyes burned, and he didn't even try to stop the tears as they blurred his eyes and ran down his cheeks. Max reached his arms out toward his daughter, the daughter he'd never even known he had. When she stepped into them, sobs racked his lungs. He held her tightly, his hands touching her hair, her shoulders. She was real. He had a daughter, and she had her arms wrapped around him just as tightly.

When he managed to blink his eyes clear, Sarah

was watching them. There had been a hardness and desperation to her face when he'd first opened the door, but now he could see she was getting just as emotional as he was. His heart reached out for her. Not just his wolf, not just the animal side of him that was bonded to her forever, but the very human side that'd been so hurt by her absence.

Letting go of Ava, he pulled Sarah into his arms and felt her hot tears sink through his shirt.

6

SARAH CLOSED HER EYES AND FOCUSED ON JUST HOW good it felt to lay her cheek against Max's broad chest again. Even his scent was the same: bergamot and citrus buried in cedar and sage. She felt her body relax, melting into his.

Her wolf had guided her way to the Glenwood packhouse, even through the dark, overgrown woods. She'd taken one turn and then another, instinctively knowing they were heading in the right direction. It was this pull between them that twisted inside her right now, like a magnet that demanded she get as close to him as possible. For so long, the beast inside her had been on guard. It couldn't let go of that, not yet, but she felt the relief of knowing she wasn't alone.

Yanking her head up, Sarah took a deep breath and a step backward. She couldn't let herself wallow in the comforting way he felt. She couldn't even let herself take too much delight in the attractive way Max had aged. There were silver flecks in his otherwise dark stubble, which she had to admit was pretty damn sexy. She'd always loved the way his nearly black hair had contrasted with those bright blue eyes. His shoulders were wider than she remembered, his mature body no longer retaining the wiry slimness of youth. It would be so easy to fall into his arms again and never let go.

There were more important matters at hand. "Max, there's so much I need to tell you."

"Yeah." He swiped the back of his hand across his cheekbone and gave Ava a fond look. "I'd say so."

"There's a good chance that some of my pack followed us. They've probably figured out by now that we're gone, and this very well may be one of the first places they look." She swallowed, hating that she had to put him in a position of immediately agreeing to protect them. He'd been her mate, and he was Ava's father. She'd always felt safe with the Glenwoods, and she'd hoped beyond all hope that they would help, but she still understood just how unfair this was.

Max's jaw flexed as he turned to flick the dead-bolt on the front door. He moved past Ava and yanked the curtains shut on the front window. "You know you don't have anything to worry about here. If that bastard is even brave enough to show up, he's not getting in."

She wanted to believe him. After all, that was exactly why she'd headed for the Glenwood pack-house. But Edward had been unstoppable up to that point. He'd managed to keep her locked away, and nothing had changed his mind. He would undoubt-edly see her escape as yet another defiance and feel the need to avenge it. Sarah glanced at Ava and the dark shadows that'd formed under her eyes. "Thank you."

"Sit down." He ushered them into the living room and perched himself on the edge of a wing-back chair. He braced his elbows on his legs and leaned forward, watching them both intensely. "There's so much I want to know. I don't really know where to start, but we have to start somewhere. Edward came to me the night you disappeared and told me that he'd had you killed. Where has he been keeping you all this time? And why?"

"In the basement of the Greystone packhouse." Somehow, saying it aloud made it much worse than just knowing it. Perhaps it was because she was telling him. Sarah sniffled and straightened up on the loveseat where she'd settled next to Ava. "As for why, I really can't say. He told me you were under the impression that I was dead, and many times since then, I've wondered why he didn't kill me. It isn't because he has a soft spot for me; I can tell you that much."

He cursed under his breath, an oath that Sarah thought she recognized but couldn't quite hear clearly. His hands curled into fists. "I'll never understand that bastard. Sorry." He directed this last part toward Ava.

"Oh, you don't have to apologize," she said, shaking her head. "He's not my grandfather, not as far as I'm concerned."

"Right." He took a controlled breath that almost sounded like a growl when he let it out.

Sarah knew what that meant. He always did that when he was pissed. Not that she blamed him. If she wasn't so exhausted from their hasty escape, she'd be pissed right now too. Sarah bit her lip. There was something else she needed to ask him, though it made her uneasy. As soon as she and Ava had started concocting their scheme, she knew there was some risk to it.

Then there were the risks of being caught, killed, or ruining someone's life by showing up. What if Max had moved on? She couldn't expect him to be alone for the rest of his life. They were true mates, and of that she had no doubt, but she wouldn't blame him in the least if he'd found someone who brought him happiness. She still needed to ask about Hunter, another question that made her nervous in a different way, but she'd start here for now. "Max, I really don't mean to intrude on your life. I know it's been a long time, and I don't expect anything."

His gaze had been on Ava still, taking her in as though he could hardly believe she was real, but his eyes snapped to Sarah's so quickly that her tongue stilled. "You're not intruding, Sarah. I wouldn't want you to go anywhere else for help. I'm still blown away by all of this, and I know there are things I should be doing, but I'm still trying to wrap my head around it." He put his hands on the arms of the chair as though he was about to get up, but he only patted his palms against the upholstery.

"Did I hear someone at the door?" Joan swept into the room from the hallway. "I thought it might be Ellen swinging by to drop off a book she was going to lend me, and—Sarah?" She stopped dead in her tracks as soon as she came far enough into the room to see who was sitting on the loveseat.

"Joan." Sarah felt her lips trembling all over again. Joan Glenwood had always been so sweet and welcoming. In fact, her warm attitude had made Sarah feel guilty time and again that Max had never been able to experience the same thing at the packhouse where she'd grown up. Over the years, she'd come to think of Joan as a second mother. Slowly, her limbs threatening to give way after such a long run, she stood. "Hi."

"Is this possible?" Joan took a hesitant step forward, the flowing sleeves of her deep purple dress falling back as she lifted her hands up to Sarah's face and rested her fingers on her cheeks. "I know that I have some crazy dreams, but this feels awfully real."

"It's real." Sarah touched Joan's wrists. "It's a long story, but it's real."

"It's not all that long, really," Max snarled. "That bastard has been keeping her prisoner this whole time. Her, as well as our daughter, Ava."

"Daughter?" Joan's eyes widened as she took in the teenager. "Daughter! Oh, there's no doubting it, is there? Come here, you sweet thing! Let me see you! But what's this?" Her eyes darkened as she saw the thick metal collars.

"They're made of a silver alloy. They keep us from shifting. It's why I was never able to reach out and contact Max telepathically, and it helped hold up Edward's false story that I was dead." Sarah's shoulders suddenly felt heavier than ever. She was used to the weight of the collar, but the burden of it now was so much more than that.

Max stood up and came over to look for himself. "They wouldn't shift along with you. They'd just cut straight through if you went into your other form," he concluded.

"Nasty things," Joan hissed as she peered around the side of Sarah's neck. "Soldered on, too. We've got to get those off right away."

"Dad might have something," Max suggested, his frown deep with disapproval. "Maybe a grinding disc or something. That metal is thick, so it's going to take a while."

Sarah felt a renewed sense of shame. It wasn't her fault. She hadn't asked for any of this, but she was literally a wild animal caught in a trap, relying on someone else's kindness to be saved.

"No need for any of that, nor to wait for another second!" Joan announced. She flapped her elbows as she brought Ava and Sarah to stand next to one another. "I can take care of it on my own."

"Mom, are you sure?" Max asked.

"Trust me, darling. If I didn't have enough power to do it before, I do now. Emotions can feed into our magic, and I've got plenty of them going. I've just got to find the weakness in the metal, and it's done for." Joan stepped up to Ava. She bent her elbow so that her hand was straight up in the air, her palm just in front of the silver collar. Her fingers were relaxed and slightly curled, but her thumb slowly moved back and forth.

Sarah watched as the tiny muscles around Joan's eyes worked, undoubtedly seeing things that Sarah herself had no hope of seeing. Soon, she would have to tell Joan that Ava had inherited a family trait from her. In fact, Ava was probably geeking out over this right now if she wasn't too exhausted to enjoy it.

After a few long moments, Joan bent her thumb all the way down and then flicked it forward. Two hot red stripes formed on the sides of Ava's collar a second before it split in half and clattered to the floor. Ava lifted her hands to her neck and touched her bare skin, smiling.

Sarah's heart surged, and she thought she might cry all over again. Right now, though, Joan had stepped over to work on her collar, and she knew she needed to be still. She watched and waited as Joan performed the same movement. Max's mother had aged, just as the rest of them had, but she'd done it gracefully. The last traces of blonde in her hair had now all gone to gray, but her eyes were still bright and vibrant. Her skin wasn't as tight as it used to be, but it was smooth and soft.

She had to wonder what Joan would think of her. Was she angry with her for leaving that day? For leaving Max? For leaving Hunter? Sarah's throat tightened at that last thought. She hadn't brought him up yet, afraid that perhaps Hunter wouldn't want her in his life. Max hadn't mentioned him, either. Was he trying to protect his son? She wanted nothing more than to hold her baby boy in her arms once again.

The snap of heat was brief, and the two thick thuds that each half made on the floor were the sound of her freedom. "Thank you," she managed, knowing that those two simple words didn't even begin to explain how grateful she was to be rid of that terrible thing.

"Of course, my darling. Of course." Joan gathered both Sarah and Ava into her arms and hugged them so tightly. "I only wish I could've done it long ago."

"Dad?"

The voice that came from the kitchen was too

deep, but it could only belong to one person. Sarah lifted her head as a young man came jogging in. He moved with the ease and grace of a shifter comfortable in his own body and the confidence of a teenage boy.

"What's going on? We heard some thumping around up here." Hunter, her baby boy, turned his head and looked into her eyes.

She didn't expect him to know her or recognize her. She couldn't even expect him to love her, not the same way he would've if she'd been around all these years. It was a pain she would carry with her forever, but as Joan's arms dropped away and Sarah crossed the room, none of that mattered. She walked slowly up to Hunter, wondering if Max had felt the same way when he'd seen Ava. It felt almost impossible for Hunter to exist like this. Her mind still categorized him as just a baby, and logic hadn't ever been able to completely correct that. "Hunter?"

He looked down at her in utter confusion. "Yeah?"

"I just..." She thought her heart might explode as she tried to wrap her brain around the fact that this boy—this young man—was her Hunter. Sarah wrapped her arms around him.

He stumbled backward as she leaned into him.

"Um, Dad?" His voice rumbled in his chest, the same way his father's did.

"Hunter, this is your mother. This is Sarah," Max said behind her.

"I'm sorry." She was crying so hard now that she couldn't even open her eyes, and the air moving through her lungs was the only noise. "I'm so sorry, baby. I'm so sorry."

"It's...it's okay." He rested an arm against her shoulder.

Sarah didn't know if Max and Joan had encouraged him to do so, or if the gesture had just been one of kindness to a strange weeping woman clinging to him for dear life. She was just so grateful to have him back.

"I think we should all go into the kitchen and find something for Sarah and Ava to eat," Joan said softly. "I can't say I'd mind a bit of a snack myself."

Sarah's feet moved toward the kitchen in the small river of shifters that'd accumulated there. She was so tired. She was so...everything. Gentle hands guided her into a chair, and someone put a mug of coffee in her hands a few minutes later. Tissues had appeared from somewhere, and she mopped her face.

When her eyes were clear enough to see, she

looked around. This was all so very normal to most people. At one point, it'd felt that way to her, too. Right now, though, it was a foreign idea to be in the main living area of a home and be a welcome visitor instead of an outcast and servant. Would she ever feel *normal* again?

She had no idea what was ahead for her life and Ava's. As long as she could avoid her father, she knew it had to be better than what they'd known.

7

"THAT'S SOME WILD SHIT."

Joan gave her grandson a look. "As much as I'd like to correct your language at the table, I have to agree with you. Sarah, I'm so sorry you had to go through that. Sitting here and trying to explain it all must not have been easy, either."

Empty plates were scattered around the table, surrounded by glasses and mugs, and a few stray napkins were crumpled here and there. The light overhead cast a yellow glow, making everything look artificial against the midnight darkness outside. Max couldn't stop staring at them. Every time he blinked, he thought he might wake up and discover it was all just a dream.

"That's okay." Sarah's eyes were swollen from

crying, though the tears had stopped for now. She fiddled with a napkin in her lap. She'd eaten two plates of food, as had Ava. "I know I'll have a lot more explaining to do. It isn't something that could just be summed up in a few sentences."

"That's understandable," Rex replied. He and Lori had been asked to join them so they'd be brought up to speed. "While it's going to take a little time to decide what to do about the Greystones, know that you and Ava are welcome to stay here at the packhouse as long as you'd like."

"Thank you."

"Of course. All right, time to get some shut-eye." Rex stood and pulled Lori's chair out for her. "Just rest assured that you have our protection."

"If there's anything you need, anything at all, we're more than happy to help." Lori studied them both with pitying eyes before following her mate back to bed.

Max's wolf writhed inside him at the idea of being away from Sarah for more than a few minutes. He wanted to have her close, and he didn't need anyone hanging around and staring at them. "Actually, Sarah, l think you and I need to do a lot of talking in private."

"Good idea." Joan stood and began clearing the

dishes from the table. Max, why don't you and Sarah go back to your place. Ava and Hunter can stay here with me. I need some time with my grandchildren." She caught Max's eyes as she crossed behind Sarah's chair and winked.

He didn't need his mother's help with this, but at least he knew he wasn't being completely unreasonable.

Sarah reached over and touched her daughter's hand. "Only if that's all right with you, honey. I'm not going to leave you unless you're okay with it."

Ava had every reason to insist she stay with her mother. From what Max could tell, Sarah was the only person she'd ever been able to trust. A tired smile crept across Ava's face as she looked at her newfound brother and grandmother. "Yeah. I'll be fine, Mom."

"I'll get you set up for the night, and you'll have the best guest room we've got," Joan insisted.

"Hey, that room's nicer than the one I've got at home," Hunter grumbled.

"I wouldn't complain if I were you," Joan reprimanded gently.

"Um, could I take a shower before I go to bed?" Ava asked politely.

"Of course. As a matter of fact, you can soak in my jacuzzi tub." With the dishes cleared, Joan took Ava's hand. "I've got more bubble bath and essential oils than an old lady has any right to, but there's not much that a good soak in a big tub can't fix. Hunter, can you head to the linen closet and start getting the room ready? I'll see if I can round up some fresh clothes for Ava."

A short time later, Max was backing out of the driveway with Sarah in the passenger seat. "You don't have to worry about her, you know. She's safe."

"I know." Sarah sighed and propped her head on her hand. "Or at least the logical part of me knows that. But Max, I really need you to understand how bad things are. As awful as my father was back in the day, he's only gotten worse."

He adjusted his grip on the steering wheel and focused hard on the road before him. "What do you mean?"

"This isn't just an enraged father who thinks his daughter is making the wrong decision. I thought he was just being overprotective when he didn't want us to get together, but it's turned into so much more than that. Everything has to be his way, and his demands go far beyond anything reasonable."

"As evidenced by the fact that he kept you and our daughter locked in a basement all this time." He wasn't sure how much more of this his wolf could take. Max felt it snarling, angry, ready to kill. "That wouldn't happen without support from the rest of them, Sarah. Rex and I are getting together in the morning to come up with a plan. I'm going to take them down and make them pay for what they've done." He could taste the blood already. It'd been a while since he'd had a good fight, and the training sessions with the younger wolves didn't count. The Greystones wouldn't get away with this.

"No, you can't do that," she said quickly, surprising him.

"Why the hell not?" His anger was boiling now, and he tried to rein it in. "I know they're your family, Sarah, but you can't just forgive and forget."

"I'm not," she insisted, "but if you go and attack the packhouse, innocent lives will be lost. Edward runs the pack like a dictator. Anyone who doesn't do exactly what he asks and when meets his wrath. I don't think my mom agreed with what he was doing, but she was terrified of what would happen if she went against him. I don't even want to think about what wrongs he may have committed that I don't even know about."

Frustration piled on top of his anger. How could anything like this have happened? And how could he not want to run right out and snap Edward Greystone's neck? Sarah needed him, though. They may have spent a long time apart, but that much he knew was true. She'd come straight to him as soon as she could. He had to take some comfort in that as he pulled into the garage at his place.

"I know you're tired," he said as they headed into the kitchen. "I am, too, but I don't think there's any way I can sleep right now. Not with all of this swirling in my head."

"I know." She followed him into the living room, her eyes sweeping over the place as they went.

She looked like an animal that'd just escaped from a zoo and didn't quite understand she was free. It hurt him all over again. "There's nothing to worry about. I told Rex we were leaving, and Glenwood wolves are on alert all over this neighborhood. If anyone so much as looks at this house funny, they'll get taken down. I don't think he's going to do anything, though."

"You don't know him that well." Sarah sank slowly onto the couch. "He's relentless, and he's not going to just let this go. He told me countless times how much I'd tarnished his honor, and I think he'd be happy to get his revenge."

His guts twisted and rebelled. Max leaned against the mantel as his mind went to war with itself. He wanted to ignore her requests to leave the Greystones alone and go take care of this problem. He'd burn their whole damn packhouse down to the ground. Another part of him wanted only to hold her and do everything she asked, anything that would give her even the slightest sense of comfort. She deserved that. He beat himself up for allowing this to happen, yet he knew it wasn't his fault. "If he's so dangerous, how did you manage to get away?" He hadn't wanted to press her when she'd first shown up, knowing all this was more than anyone should be expected to handle. He had to know, though.

One side of her mouth quirked up slightly as she met his eyes. "Ava."

"Really?" Even though he'd never known his daughter until now, pride bloomed inside him. "What did she do?"

"Your eyes aren't the only thing she inherited from your side. She's like Dawn and your mother." A hint of energy returned to Sarah's face.

"You mean..." He hadn't even had the chance to

consider it. It shouldn't really be that much of a surprise, considering the witch bloodline was so prominent among the women in his family. Still, knowing that something so remarkable had sparked in such a horrible place had more magic to it than any spell.

Sarah was smiling fully now. "I may have helped with some of the logistics, but it was really all her." She went on to explain how Ava's skills had made all the difference in finally breaking them free from the Greystones' clutches.

"That's incredible. I grew up with witches all around me, but I never thought magic would make such a difference in my life." Max ran a hand through his hair, incredulous.

"I knew she had some powers," Sarah admitted. "She'd discovered a few things she could do when she was small, but I didn't think it would ever turn into anything major. Not without help from someone who understood it, anyway. I guess growing up the way she did, she learned how to keep things a secret, even from me. I only just found out how much she could do."

"Wow." He pushed himself away from the fireplace and came to stand closer to her. "I want to ask you so many things, and that was why we came here, but I feel like I could talk to you for a year straight and still not get it all out."

"I want to tell you everything, but it's hard to know where to begin. As I said, it's not something I can put into simple terms. Not any of it." Her eyes were roving the room again. "I like your place."

"Thanks." Could he tell her how good it felt to have her there with him? This had been his home for years, a place he'd chosen because it had a big backyard for Hunter to grow up in, and it wasn't too far from the packhouse.

She pointed to the green glass swag light hanging in the corner. "That surprises me, though. You never liked that old stuff."

"It came with the place." The answer was honest, but it didn't tell her everything. He'd walked through the house with the real estate agent, knowing he was buying it for himself, but he wanted to think Sarah would've approved of it. Moving out on his own was something he'd done because he'd felt he should, but he'd dragged himself through the process. Nothing had excited him then, not when he'd just lost his mate.

That swag light, though, had felt like a beacon from Sarah from beyond the grave. "I left it because I remembered going to all those flea markets and tag sales with you. It was the same sort of junk you would've brought home."

"It's not junk!" She laughed as she crossed the living room to get a better look at it. "They don't make things like they used to."

"With bad wiring, you mean?" He'd moved up behind her, and when she turned to argue with him, he caught her in his arms. Her curves fit in his embrace just as they always had, sending thrills through his body and driving his wolf into a frenzy all over again. "Sarah, I think the pain of knowing you were alive this whole time is even worse than the pain of thinking you were dead. I can't tell you how sorry I am."

"You don't have anything to be sorry for." Her eyes were liquid and sweet as they looked up at his, soft and alluring. She traced her fingertips over his shirt sleeve, slowly touching, exploring.

"I do. I'm going to protect you this time. I'll promise I'll never let you go again." He bent his head and pressed his lips against hers. It should've felt strange or awkward after all these years, but it was like coming home. A contentment he'd been missing for so long washed over him as she lifted herself toward him.

His hands swerved along the curve of her hips and around to her back, lowering slightly as he pulled her closer. A vibration of pleasure escaped from his throat as she parted her lips. He dipped the tip of his tongue into her depths, finding the silky warmth of her tongue waiting for him. A part of him had died when he thought she had, but it was coming back to life.

Sarah's hands moved up his biceps to his shoulders, tracing the broad planes there. As her touch moved up the back of his neck, she bent her fingers and grazed her nails gently through his short hair. Her body pressed against his, her breasts compressing softly against his chest.

Anticipation built inside him as he remembered just how good her skin had felt against his. He worked his fingers between the hem of her shirt and the waistband of her jeans, digging his fingers into the softness of her backside, and he knew he was done for. He didn't just need her or want her. They were meant to be. The universe had dictated it a long time ago, and no one could keep them apart this time.

She stretched herself up toward him, leaning her weight into him as her caresses fluttered around his neck and the graying stubble along his jawline.

Sarah touched him, taking him all in, delighting in him. Her palms drifted down his firm chest and stomach until she was twisting her hands in the hem of his shirt.

The beast inside him took over. His longing for her buzzed in his ears and drowned out the rest of the world as he scooped her off her feet. Her weight was easy in his arms, natural, as though it had always belonged there, and he carried her into his bedroom.

Sarah clung to him as they moved, her arms desperate for him. She trusted him; he could feel it in the ease with which they'd come together.

Max laid her down on the bed, eager to satiate his craving for her. He stripped her of her shirt, dragging his lips down her neck and into the hollow between her breasts. As he slid her jeans down over her hips, he delighted in the softness of her thighs. She had changed, yes, but she was still the same luscious woman he'd fallen for so long ago.

The floodgates of his desire opened as Sarah's hands eagerly pulled at his shirt, belt, and jeans, her fingers running alongside his spine. Her legs moved against his, skimming, touching, inviting.

He'd missed her. He'd longed for her. He'd hoped but never thought it could be real, and now there she was, right with him where she belonged. His soul was ablaze as Max sank into her heat. He slowly pushed deeper and then stopped, holding himself there just so he could close his eyes and revel in the way they fit together.

Her legs slid around his, her toes locking in the crook of his ankles as she undulated beneath him. Her hands and lips roved over him, taking him in every way she possibly could. She bucked her hips in rhythm with his, grinding against him until she was throwing her head back into the pillow.

Her breath became nothing more than short gasps, and Max could feel her contracting around his shaft, driving him toward the edge as she approached it herself. He wanted to hold back, to keep this moment for as long as he could, but she felt too damn good. His body tightened when Sarah's lips found his again. She stiffened and then cried out, her core pulling him in, welcoming him, demanding him. Her groan of satisfaction echoed in his mouth, and the desire he tasted on her tongue shot through him, beckoning his own release.

Max held her there on top of the covers as reality slowly slipped back in around them. He could hear the clock ticking on the wall and the gentle swoosh of the ceiling fan. Most of all, though, he could hear her breathing as she lay there in his arms. Her heart-beat was a welcome thrum against his chest. A tear heated the corner of his eye and slid down toward the mattress, and he let it go. Destiny and fate had never meant so much to him.

8

"So, you've really never been in your wolf form before?" Hunter arched a brow toward his newfound sister.

"Never."

"Weird. Well, you're gonna love it. Once you get through a few shifts, you'll have to start coming out with us to train."

Sarah slid her eyes over and shared a secret smile with Max as they walked out into the woods behind the Glenwood packhouse with their children. She hadn't had much time to contemplate what it might be like for Hunter and Ava to finally meet or how well they might get along. So far, though, so good.

Things between herself and Max were certainly

good, maybe even better after what happened last night. God, it'd been so long. She still held the memories of making love to him before, but nothing compared to the way their bodies felt together in the flesh. It had never been an act to satisfy a physical need with him. It was a deeper hunger, a longing for not just each other's bodies but each other's souls.

But after sixteen years of celibacy, her body sure didn't mind the attention. Right now, though, it'd have to wait. Sarah turned her focus back to the kids.

Ava wasn't much younger than Hunter, but her lack of life experience meant she was already looking up to him. "I don't think I'll be ready for that anytime soon. You guys have been training together all this time, and I haven't even shifted before."

Hunter could've been jealous by suddenly being forced to share the attention with a younger sibling. Instead, he'd taken her under his wing. "So? You're still one of us, and I'm sure you'll get used to it in no time. You'll catch up. Don't worry."

"They're kind of cute, aren't they?" Sarah kept her voice down so only Max would hear.

"Definitely." His head was back, his face toward the sun, and he'd been smiling the entire time. "I'm glad to see you're okay with being out here."

Her stomach shivered a bit, and Sarah realized

she'd actually relaxed enough to enjoy herself for a moment. She'd been trapped in her father's house for so long, and every time she even thought about walking out the door, it was impossible not to imagine the Greystones coming for her once again. As those thoughts tried to creep back in, she shoved them away. She couldn't live her life like that. She had to be strong for Ava, no matter how hard it might be. "I'm working on it. It helps to know so many others are around, ready to jump in if needed. I don't want anyone to put their life on the line for me, but—"

"Hey." He moved closer and slid his hand down her forearm and wrist until their fingers were clasped. "They will, whether you ask them to or not. You're one of us, and that's how we do things. You know that. It's exactly why you and Ava are staying here at the packhouse; it's easier to keep you safe until we know where this is going."

She nodded and clamped her lips around further protests. How could she argue against them helping her when that was the exact reason she'd come to them? "I guess I'm just saying I appreciate it."

He'd been looking around and ahead, but now his eyes met hers. "I'm hoping this is just a temporary situation, though, and that you and Ava will move in with Hunter and I once we know things are safe. I need you by my side again, Sarah."

The shiver that moved through her now wasn't one of fear but pure pleasure. She'd had no idea how he might receive her after all these years, but so far, he'd welcomed her with open arms. Too much had happened over the years for them to pick up exactly where they left off, but it was easy to fall for him all over again. "I think we can make that happen. First, I'll have to figure out if I still know how to shift."

The trail had opened up into a clearing, and Max brought the group to a stop. "I'm sure it'll come back to you, just like riding a bike."

"I don't know if I remember how to do that, either!" Sarah laughed. The breeze rustled the leaves on the trees and brought the scent of wildflowers. Birds sang as they lived their own lives overhead. It was all so bright and picturesque that it was hard to believe this was real. "Ava, are you ready for this?"

The girl pulled in a breath and puffed her cheeks out as she let it go. "I don't know. I'm not sure what to do."

"That's all right," Max said gently. "We all have to learn at some point. It might be a little hard at first, but once you get it down, it'll get faster and easier every time you do it."

"Okay." She looked doubtful as she shifted her feet in the grass.

"You can feel your wolf inside you, right?"

She nodded.

"It wants to come out. I can promise you that even if it's never been out before, it's interested. That's just the nature of the beast. All you have to do is let it. Our human side is what keeps it in check, so this is about letting go of that and tuning in to your wild self. Does that make sense?"

Sarah watched as Max coached their daughter. He'd only known her for a couple of days, but he was no stranger to being a father. She hated that he'd had to take care of Hunter on his own, but he'd obviously done well.

"I want you to close your eyes and concentrate on your wolf," Max continued. Take a deep breath, and when you let it out, just imagine your entire human self melting away. Visualize your wolf breaking out into the world."

"Okay." Ava did as she was told. Her brows crunched together as she tried to concentrate. She took that deep breath, and nothing happened.

"Try relaxing your shoulders as you let your

breath out. Just let your whole body sag," Max suggested.

Ava gave a subtle nod before she tried again. Her shoulders sagged and her knees bent. Her hands dangled at her sides, and she even let her head fall back on her neck, but her wolf refused to come out.

"Don't worry," Max intoned gently. "Just relax and know that this will come."

But Ava's eyes were open now, and tears were swimming in them. "I don't know that it will."

"Sure it will." Hunter stepped in now, eager to offer some guidance. "Like Dad said, though, make sure you relax. Getting all tense and stressed out will make it harder."

Max gave him a look of pride, but the glare from Ava was one that suited a younger sister who didn't want advice from her older brother just now.

"Easy for you to say," she grumbled. "You get to do it all the time."

"Sweetie, it's all right." Sarah hated this for her. She knew how important this was. Ava needed to know the side of her that'd been so imprisoned that even she hadn't seen it. "It does sound easy for those who get to do it on a regular basis. It feels hard for you right now, but it won't always be. We're here for you. Why don't you just give it one more shot, and then you can take a break for a bit."

She still looked doubtful, but Ava nodded. She closed her eyes, relaxed, and grew limp. Sarah bit her lip when she saw nothing happening, but then her heart shot up into her throat when she spotted Ava's hand. Her short fingernails had suddenly turned into thick, dark claws.

"Ow!" Ava screamed. She yanked her hand up to her face, staring wide-eyed at what she'd just done. "You didn't tell me it would hurt that bad!"

"It won't always," Max hurried to tell her. "I'm sorry. At this point, I don't even remember it hurting. You'll get there, too."

"Try again," Hunter encouraged. "I bet you can do even more next time."

The claws had retreated, leaving human finger-nails behind, and Ava shook her head. "I think I'm good for now."

"I'll go," Sarah volunteered, figuring Ava probably wanted some of the attention off of her. She might not have grown up like other girls her age, but she was still a teenager.

"Are you sure you want to, Mom? It doesn't feel good," Ava cautioned.

"I know." Sarah gently laid her hand on Ava's

cheek. She was such a sweet girl, despite all that had happened to her. "But your dad is right. Even though it hurts at first, it won't always. I know it didn't hurt when I used to shift all the time. It probably won't be that great for me at first, but I've got to get it over with."

Max gave her an approving look and nodded.

There was no need for anyone to give her advice or guidance. Though she hadn't experienced her wolf in many years, this wasn't the same as coaching someone new to it. Unlike Ava, Sarah knew what she was missing. Still, she followed the guidance that Max had given Ava. Her lungs filled, and she consciously forced her muscles to relax. It was like shrugging off your human form to let out the beast representing your true self. But it'd been so long. Sarah felt like she was reaching into a past that didn't exist anymore, like trying to recreate childhood memories.

It wasn't easy, though she hadn't expected it to be. Her human side had kept her wolf locked away for the last sixteen years, making it far stronger than the beast that lived inside of her. Sarah could feel the barrier between the two sides of her, thick and resistant. If she was honest with herself, she was scared, but she was born a wolf shifter. This needed to happen, and there was no point in waiting. She forced another breath in and out.

It'd been hesitant at first, not sure if there was a pathway out. When she summoned it a second time, her wolf came ripping out of her. She felt her skin give way to thousands of hairs, making a thick fur sprout all over her body. Excruciating pain blistered her skull and seared through her body as her bones twisted and bent, conforming her to the new shape. A thunderous sound filled her ears as they moved higher up on her head, and she felt just as much as heard the bones cracking in her face as her muzzle stretched out. Sarah's body twisted and writhed, making her completely lose any orientation or balance. She fell forward, but her paws caught her just before her face hit the ground.

Slowly, Sarah pushed herself upright on all fours, blinking as she looked down at her body. Sleek silver fur covered her chest and legs. The grass felt cool and comforting beneath her paw pads, and her tail was a natural extension of her body. Everything she'd already noticed about the day was suddenly enhanced several times over. A squirrel moved through the underbrush on the other side of the clearing. Turning, she could see it clearly. It paused, knowing danger was near. Excitement filled her blood.

You look beautiful.

That voice in her head was one she never thought she'd hear again. Sarah turned away from the squirrel to see that Max had shifted as well. Damn, he was handsome in either form he took. His fur was slightly darker than most of the Glenwoods, his eyes still as bright as they were in his human form. He was strong and muscular, sure on his feet. *I'm sure that shift wasn't too beautiful.*

Does it really matter? He moved a couple of steps closer. *You did it, and I'm glad. I've missed this so much.*

Sarah closed her eyes as she felt the deep comfort of having her mate again. Being cut off from him was one of the cruelest punishments Edward could've given her, other than forcing her daughter to live the same life. Perhaps that was exactly why he'd done it. He'd known just how much it would hurt, and that was what he was after. *Me, too.*

"No, you really can't compare yourself to anyone else," Hunter said, and Sarah turned to see that he was still trying to coach Ava. "Just because your mom—our mom—did it that quickly doesn't mean you're doing anything wrong. It's just going to take some time."

Now that Ava's here, I can see he's actually been listening to me all these years. Max's voice was amused as the two wolves took a short walk around the perimeter of the clearing. *I swear I've told him the exact same things when it comes to training. He's always thought he ought to be able to get the hang of everything right away. Eventually, he realizes he just has to put the time in.*

I'm sure Ava will figure it out, too. Sarah glanced at her daughter, who was kicking her toe in the grass but nodding and responding as Hunter spoke to her. Her heart hurt for her. No, her heart hurt for both of them. They were her babies, and they'd been done wrong. There was nothing she could do to fix any of it, other than try her best to make things better as they all went forward. Would it be enough?

You don't have to worry about them.

Sarah startled. *Sorry. It's been an awfully long time since I had anyone in my head. I forgot to filter.*

There's nothing to be sorry about at all. I like hearing it. And really, they're going to be all right. Ava will find her wolf, and both of them will get used to having two parents instead of just one. Everything will be just fine.

I hope so. She wanted so badly for things to be okay, but it was a little hard for her to see still. It wasn't easy to just completely change gears and start living her life as a free person. Her children mattered most, and she had to be strong for them. If they believed that *she* believed everything was okay, then it would be. *I think I ought to change back and give Ava another chance, if she wants it.*

Yeah. His eyes met hers, drinking in that one last, long moment in this form.

Shivers rippled down her spine. Sarah didn't want to change back. She wanted to turn and run through the woods, to bound from one side of the trail to the other and explore the capabilities of this body that she'd been denied. Most of all, she wanted to keep Max right there in her head. The universe had bound their hearts a long time ago, and she liked the comfort of having him at her side. That would have to wait until later.

Just as slowly as she'd become her wolf, Sarah packed it away. It resisted at first, having enjoyed this freedom, but she knew it'd be coming out again soon. Again, she lost her balance as she transitioned from four feet to two, but Max was there to catch her. She smiled up at him. "Thanks."

"Of course."

9

MAX SAT ON THE BACK PORCH, RESTING COMFORTABLY in an Adirondack chair. The view from there was stunning, overlooking the backyard and out into the woods. When was the last time he'd actually just sat down and enjoyed it? He couldn't remember. Nor could he remember the last time he'd felt so damn content. There had to be a certain amount of peace in a man if he could just sit and watch the world around him instead of getting things done or worrying about the future. Having Sarah around made every day feel like a slow Sunday morning, the kind where no plans were made or needed. It felt good, but strange.

There were a lot of things Max had been realizing about himself over the last several days. All of his attention should've been on Sarah and Ava, considering everything they'd been through and that they weren't completely out of the woods yet. But his mind kept twisting and turning, showing him new perspectives and making him think about himself more than he'd care to.

One of those realizations was that he'd never truly been relaxed since the Greystones had taken Sarah from him. He'd constantly carried a tension around, never at peace with the idea that she was dead and that he could do nothing about it. The fact that his wolf had nudged him now and then had kept him from moving on with his life, and now, he couldn't be happier that things had worked out that way.

He just had to figure out how to move on from here.

"Here you go."

A mug of coffee appeared in his hands. Max looked down inside the mug, spotting the perfect shade of deep caramel. He took a slow sip. "No sugar."

"Just the way you like it." Sarah took the seat next to him. "Or at least, that's the way I remember you liking it."

"Nothing's changed." He rested the mug on the

arm of the chair as he studied her. Would he ever get used to having her there? Or knowing she was alive? Max couldn't help but marvel over the way time had changed her, yet hadn't. There were a few silver strands in her hair, but overall, it was just as soft and brilliant as he remembered. Those were the same brown eyes that'd haunted his dreams, but the skin wasn't quite as tight around them. Then there were those curves of hers. He'd already devoured them during the one chance they'd had to get a little time alone. Her stomach was softer, her breasts and hips rounder, but they'd driven him just as wild as ever. No. Nothing had changed.

She wrapped her hands around her mug as she looked out over the yard. "I found myself just making it that way for you, but then I wasn't sure. It's kind of funny how those old habits are taking over again."

He could think of some old habits he wouldn't mind starting up, like having her in his bed every night. It only made sense for Sarah and Ava to stay at the packhouse where they'd be safest, so Max and Hunter were doing the same for now. But Max knew Sarah needed some space, and it hadn't felt right to just assume. He looked forward to sharing a bed again, falling asleep with the warmth of her back against his chest, her ass pressed against him. He felt a tightness in his jeans at the thought and knew it would have to wait until later. Searching his brain for what they'd just been discussing, he shook his head. "The coffee is just fine."

"I know it's already getting close to lunch, but I needed another caffeine boost," she explained.

He was on the alert again now, watching her. Was there something he'd missed? "Are you not sleeping well?"

She watched a bird fly overhead and then looked down into her mug. "I'm just worried. Everything feels so perfect right now, like a fantasy. I'm waiting for the other shoe to drop, but I don't want Ava to feel like there's anything wrong. I don't know. I guess I'm just adjusting, and it's wearing me out mentally and emotionally."

"That's understandable." In fact, it sounded an awful lot like what was happening in his own mind. His thoughts were spinning, and he was constantly trying to look at things from all angles. Max wanted every single bit of information, even though he couldn't be entirely sure what that information was. It didn't help that Edward hadn't shown up yet. He knew that wasn't like the old bastard, and it made him wonder what Greystone was plotting. Max had stayed up late several nights, talking to Rex and Brody. They'd assured him everything would be fine, but nothing would be good enough for Max until he knew that Edward wasn't a problem anymore. He'd already been enough of a problem in the past, which was haunting him a bit right now, too. "Can I ask you a question?"

She rolled a shoulder. "Of course."

There was so much for them to talk about, and he'd let that be an excuse not to bring this up until now. As far as Max was concerned, it couldn't wait any longer. He had to know. "How do you feel about Ava's magic?"

Sarah blinked.

"The witch bloodline in my family was why your father never wanted us to be together," he went on. "Honestly, I was never sure where you stood on that. Knowing that it's only shown up in females meant it was never an issue when it came to Hunter. Ava is clearly another matter."

She rubbed her thumb over the handle of her mug, smiling gently. "I'm sorry for my hesitation, but I guess you caught me off guard. I can understand why you'd ask me that, but it's just who she is. As a mother, that means I accept it as such."

Max instantly felt like an ass. Of course she

accepted it. Ava was her daughter, and Sarah had done everything she could to make sure the girl was raised decently despite her horrendous circumstances. "I shouldn't have asked."

"Yes, you should've," she insisted, turning in her chair so that she faced him more fully. "If something bothers you or you have a question, don't keep it to yourself. We have to get to know each other all over again, Max, and I don't want that to stop just because you're worried you might offend me."

He pulled in a breath, trying to find the right words. "I just know you've been in a very sensitive situation, so it makes things a little harder."

"I know." She leaned back in her chair and sighed. "I find myself wondering when things will feel less complicated, but then I remind myself that life's already a lot easier than it was a few days ago. It's hard to be patient right now."

Max couldn't agree more. He was impatient for this business with Greystone to be behind them. He'd always respected Rex and his position as Alpha, but at the moment, it felt like his older brother was moving a little too slowly while they waited for Edward's next move. He was impatient to get Sarah home with him, where the four of them could live like an actual family, the way they were always meant to. Most of all, he was impatient to settle into the relationship he knew he and Sarah could have once everything calmed down. His mate was home. She was alive. She'd given him not only a son but a *daughter*. He didn't want or need anything beyond that. "I know."

"As far as her gifts, I suppose it's a little more complicated than simply accepting them." Sarah's brows came down, and the fine lines next to her eyes deepened as she slipped into the past. "Ava surprised me with them when she was little. If she was afraid of the dark, she could create this little spark of light on the end of her finger. Or if she got particularly frustrated with something she was trying to do, this little breeze would suddenly kick up in the room, even without a window open. I came to appreciate her talent when it came to things like the light because I knew it helped her get through our confinement. It always terrified me under the surface, though, because I didn't know what Edward might do to her if he ever found out."

His teeth ground together. "I don't like to think that anyone would ever harm their own grandchild, but considering his other acts, I'm not so sure."

"Neither was I." Tears glistened in her eyes until she blinked them away. "I was constantly afraid of what might happen to her, either if he found out what she could do or if he thought that harming her might be just punishment for me."

His fist pounded into the arm of the chair, sending vibrations down through the deck beneath him as he tried to control the fury that flooded through him. "Selene's blood, I can't believe the man would be such a monster! As your mate and Ava's father, I can't even begin to tell you the things I'd like to do to him for what he's done." Max's wolf was churning inside him, ready to come out and make sure Edward never had the chance to harm anyone again.

Sarah had asked him not to do anything right now. He'd gone along with it at first, wanting to keep her happy, but there were some things a man simply had to take care of. He was just about to tell her when he saw her sag against the back of the chair, frowning down into her coffee. His anger still simmered inside him, threatening to come to an explosive boil at any moment. "I'm sorry. I know he's your father, despite everything else. I didn't mean to make you uncomfortable."

"It's fine." She lifted her head, but only to gaze off into the distance.

A vague memory tickled at the back of his mind.

Sarah wouldn't look at him when she was angry. It'd always driven him crazy. "It's not fine, clearly."

"Just let it go, Max." She turned to the right, pulling her eyes even further from him.

A different anger moved through him now. "What happened to what you said a few minutes ago? Am I the only one who should speak up when something bothers me, or does that also apply to you?" He heard the petulance in his voice, which only raised his frustration.

She whipped her head back around, her eyes glaring and her chin tipped back. Sarah looked like she was ready for a fight. In fact, she looked just the way she had that last time he'd seen her, before all of this had happened. But she flicked her fingers in the air. "You know what? Fine. I'll just say it. The part about witches and magic never bothered me, Max. It was different, but it wasn't a deal breaker by any means. I can't say that I didn't struggle with the other traditional aspects of your pack."

How easy it'd been to forget all the things they used to fight about. Max had only been concentrating on how nice it was to have her at his side where she belonged. It'd been hard to know he'd had another child, one whose life he hadn't been involved in, but knowing about Ava now had made him just as giddy as welcoming a baby into the world. He'd been letting his excitement over Sarah's arrival override the reasons they used to fight in the first place. "Like what?"

"It's been a long time, Max, but I don't think I should have to recite it all over again," she returned.

"I'd rather you did, so we can get down to the bottom of it. We've already said we have a lot of things to talk about, a lot of things to figure out. If this is one of them, we might as well get it over with." His exasperation was taking hold of him now, and he didn't want to just walk away from it and pretend it didn't exist. Max wanted to pick it apart, to find out what was wrong and dig it out like a splinter.

"You and I were raised very differently, Max. My family has a lot of problems, yes, but it's not as though I can just erase who I am and what I believe in. You guys are just so traditional, so old school. All this business about Selene and marking has never sat right with me. It feels so constrictive." She put her mug on the table next to her and ran a hand through her hair.

"You're looking at it the wrong way," he insisted. "We've been over this."

"Yes, and you were the one who just demanded that we go over it again, as I recall."

"Look, I don't want to fight with you. I just want you to understand that—" Max stopped talking as the door behind them opened.

Joan stepped out onto the deck, her eyes darting back and forth between Max and Sarah. She undoubtedly knew something was wrong, but she wasn't going to interfere. "I just came to let you know that lunch is ready. Dawn has the day off, and she and I have been busy in the kitchen."

"That sounds great." Lunch would be a nice distraction, and it would cut off the argument he was about to have with Sarah before it got any worse. He really didn't want to fight with her. They'd have to work a few things out at some point, but it was all too new to do it right now. Max stood and held out his hand. "Shall we?"

Sarah twisted her mouth as she considered it but then took his hand and let him pull her up out of the chair. "I could eat."

He gave her hand an extra tug to pull her closer as she got to her feet. His wolf reacted just as much as his human did to having her close like that.

"Do you know where Hunter and Ava are?" Joan

asked as she opened the patio door. "I haven't seen them for a bit."

Sarah's hand squeezed so that her knuckles dug into the sides of Max's fingers. "I thought they were in the basement."

"They're not," Joan confirmed.

"I'll check their rooms," Max said as they stepped inside.

"I'll double-check the basement and maybe the garage." Sarah darted off, her footsteps rattling downward.

Max headed up. He looked in Ava's room. Joan had gone all out trying to make the poor girl feel like she finally had a home. A giant stuffed panda sat on top of a fluffy purple comforter, and a stack of books rested on the nightstand. There was no sign of Ava.

Next, he popped into the room where Hunter had been staying. It hadn't been nearly as personalized since they all knew he and Max wouldn't remain at the packhouse any longer than necessary. He'd still managed to leave socks on the floor and several empty sports drink containers on the dresser, but they weren't in there, either. A quick check of the other guest rooms yielded no different results.

His feet thundered on the stairs in time with his heart. No one could've breached the packhouse and gotten to them. They had to be around somewhere. He pulled out his phone and dialed just as he hit the landing in the living room.

"Hey, Dad."

"Where are you?" Max could hear the steady whooshing of traffic in the background, and his heart rate sped up even more.

Sarah had just gotten into the living room, and she watched him with widened eyes.

"I brought Ava into town to show her around a bit. We got some ice cream, and then we were going to walk through some of the shopping areas and stuff."

Max's heart was pounding so hard now that it threatened to burst out of his chest. His wolf was on high alert. Something was wrong. Hunter was a good kid, and under normal circumstances, Max wouldn't have thought twice about the kids going into town. But these circumstances were far from normal. "I don't like this, Hunter. You two need to get in your truck right now and head back to the packhouse."

A long sigh of annoyance escaped Hunter's throat. Max could almost see him rolling his eyes and tossing his head back, knowing he had no choice but to listen. "Fine. We'll just—hey! What the

—" Thuds and scuffles came through the phone, followed by a scream.

"Hunter!" Max was already racing out the door with Sarah hot on his tail. "Hunter! Ava!"

The line disconnected just as he fired up the engine.

10

SARAH PRESSED HER HANDS TO HER FACE. MAX HAD the gas pedal pinned to the floor, and the scenery that flew past the window was nothing more than a blur. Her babies. Her sweet babies. What had happened to them? Max had told her what he'd heard, but that didn't give her any real information. The only thing she wanted was to hold them in her arms again and know they were safe.

She felt the tension crackling between them, filling the vehicle. They'd been forced to switch gears after the start of a pretty big argument. The subject at hand might be different, but she knew that nothing had really changed.

"They probably went to Vanilla Jill's." Max adjusted his hands on the wheel. "That's one of

Hunter's favorite places, and he's been excited to show Ava everything he knows. We'll start there. Try calling his phone to see if you can get him."

She picked up the device where Max had discarded it on the console. Sarah had seen plenty of people using smartphones. Everyone in the Greystone packhouse had one except for her and Ava. The mobile she'd had before she was captured was nothing more than a flip phone with a camera, and she bit her lip and forced back the tears that threatened once again. Was something as stupid as knowing how to use a smartphone really going to stand in her way?

"There's a button down on the bottom that looks like a phone." Max didn't bother flicking on his turn signal as he jetted out from behind a station wagon and zoomed around it. "Press that. Then you'll see Hunter's name. All you have to do is click on it."

Grateful that she didn't have to explain, Sarah did as he asked, leaning forward with hope. That hope didn't last long. "It went straight to his voicemail."

"It sounded like he dropped it. It probably broke." He zipped around a curve, ignoring the signs to slow down.

Sarah tipped her head back and closed her eyes as she wrapped her arms around her stomach.

"Are you all right?"

No. Of course she wasn't. Neither one of them were. "I haven't been in a car in a very long time other than the short drive to your house. I guess it's one of those things you just get used to when you do it all the time, but that tolerance goes away after a while."

"I'm sorry. I can't slow down, though." The roar of the engine underlined his statement.

"I know. And I don't want you to." The speed and movement of the car were horrendous. She didn't dare look over and see how fast they were going. The faster, the better, though. They just had to get to the kids. "I've tried so hard to raise Ava right. I gave up on getting away a long time ago. I hadn't been able to do it just for myself, and I knew I couldn't once I had a child in tow. That meant she'd never have a life of freedom like a normal person. She doesn't know to stay away from strangers on the street. She probably doesn't even know how to buy something because she's never had the chance. I've told her, but it's not the same."

Max let out a grunt. "It wasn't fair that you— either of you—had to go through that."

"No."

She dared to open her eyes and saw the stiffness in Max's spine. He'd been angry with her just a few minutes ago, irritated that she hadn't accepted his pack's traditional ways, even after all these years. He was livid now, but it felt different. Max had a way of radiating his rage and directing it at the person who was responsible. He was positively seething, but not at her.

"I wanted so much more for her. I still do. Once we got to the packhouse, I thought she'd have a chance to have that. Now, it might all be taken away from her." Sarah had been trying so hard not to let her fear grip her. She'd been fighting against herself constantly, forcing herself to remember that she had Max and the rest of the Glenwoods to help them. So far, she'd managed to contain it well enough to let Ava start getting comfortable. Perhaps she'd done too good of a job, or Ava wouldn't have just tagged along with Hunter without bothering to ask.

To her surprise, Max's hand slid over and rested in the crook of her elbow as he slowed down at the city limits. "It'll be all right."

She didn't want his platitudes right now. He couldn't know that it would be okay because she sure as hell didn't.

"It will," he insisted, even though she hadn't argued with him out loud. "Ava's at a disadvantage because of her childhood, but remember that Hunter didn't grow up that way. He's got a good head on his shoulders, and the pack's constant training means he's ready to protect her."

Sarah could appreciate the sentiment, but he was talking about a controlled situation. If someone attacked the packhouse and the Glenwoods were all on hand, she could believe they'd be ready. But what if the kids were off in town by themselves? When anyone and everyone could be an enemy? "I'm sure he's a great fighter, but I should've talked to the kids more about the danger out there now that Ava and I have escaped. I should've told them they had to stay at the packhouse no matter what."

"They both know your family is a threat. Sometimes kids go and do dumb things even when you tell them not to."

"Ava didn't have a chance for much of that," she retorted. He made it sound like it was all so easy, like kids were just going to be kids, and they had to let go of what they couldn't control. Maybe that was fine for him and Hunter, but Max just had no idea how difficult this had been. "She knew how grave our situation was. She had to listen to what I said because I was trying to keep her alive and safe. It wasn't until right before we left that she'd started doing anything the least bit disobedient, and that was more of a test of her magic than anything."

Max let out that long, breathy growl that she was so familiar with as he swiveled his head side to side, scanning the sidewalks. "I don't know why you don't think I understand that. I do. That's exactly why I'm saying that things were different for us."

Sarah pressed her lips together. Was she really being unreasonable? Was she asking too much? Hell, the only thing she wanted was to get her children back. She stopped bothering to argue for the moment while she, too, looked around. It was so strange to finally see Eugene again. She'd known the town well before, and it carried a certain sense of familiarity with it, but it was like reliving an old dream. She didn't remember that insurance office being gray, and where she expected a tiny shop, she found a parking lot instead. The sidewalk there was new, and one restaurant had been swapped out for another. It was too much like coming back to Max, where things were the same, yet not. She focused on faces, looking for any signs of her children, a struggle, or anything else that might help.

"There they are." Max yanked the vehicle over to

the side of the street, bumping the tire against the curb and barely throwing it into park before he was out the door.

Sarah shot out after him, charging up to where her kids sat on a bench. Ava's hair was tangled, and she had a scratch on her cheek. Hunter's arms were covered in smudges of dirt, and his shirt had a long rip at the bottom. Something had definitely happened, and it was more than just him dropping his phone. "Are you okay?"

"Yeah." He held up his cell to show the shattered screen. "I dropped it when they attacked."

Max looked around. "Are they still here?"

"No. They ran off that way. Since I couldn't reach you, I decided the best thing was to stay put for the moment. I would've walked over to Selene's, but I knew they weren't open yet, so Rex probably wouldn't be there."

"Good thinking. Let's get in the car." He ushered them back to the vehicle.

Sarah waited until both kids were in the back seat with their doors shut before she got in herself. She fell into her seat, exhausted and tense. "What happened?"

"We were just walking down the sidewalk, about to go check out some stores, when these two guys attacked us," Hunter explained. His eyebrows drew together as he recounted the tale, making him look even more like his father than he already did. "It caught me by surprise, and I dropped my phone. They took us down an alley, and a car was waiting down at the other end."

Sarah's nausea instantly came back. This hadn't been random.

"There was no way we were going with them. I shifted. I know I'm not supposed to do it in town and in broad daylight, but I had to. I knew it was the only way I'd be able to fight two of them off and help Ava." He lifted his chin, waiting for the lecture that would come.

"Sometimes, that's what we have to do," came Max's reply.

Hunter took that as his cue. "I was just trying to keep them away from Ava. One was coming after me, but I knew the other would get her. So I bit his ankle and held on, trying to give her a chance to run away."

"I didn't really know what to do at first," Ava cut in. Her eyes were wide and her skin was pale. She'd definitely had a scare, but there was a glimmer of something else just under the surface. "I couldn't fight them the way that Hunter had. I couldn't even try to get my wolf to come out. Something else kicked in for me instead, and I didn't have time to worry about whether or not I was going to get it wrong. I transported both of them into the dumpster."

"You should've heard them!" Hunter added, laughing now. "It was a super nasty dumpster, because we were behind a restaurant. They were screaming like babies in there! But the best part..." He trailed off now because he was laughing so hard.

Sarah didn't find any of this the least bit funny.

But Ava did. Hunter gestured at her to continue, though she was laughing almost as hard as he was. "I sent the dumpster rolling down the alley, right into their car!"

"Dude, that was the best!" Hunter held out his hand for a high-five from Ava. She stared at his hand for a second before she slapped it.

The two of them had clearly bonded over this experience, and Sarah even had to wonder if they'd rehearsed some of their tale. This wasn't all just fun and games, though, not by a long shot. "As glad as I am that the two of you have each other's backs, this isn't okay. You never should've left the house without talking to us."

Conflict moved over Hunter's face. "I'm sorry. I

just haven't had to ask permission to leave the house for quite a while."

He was right, and Sarah knew it. She hated that she didn't know how to parent her own child, not in a situation like this and not when he technically wasn't even a child anymore. "Things are different right now. Ava, you've got to be more careful than this. You don't have real-world experience, and as you've already seen, you can't shift to protect yourself yet. You can't assume you'll be safe because you're with another person."

"It was actually Ava and her magic that saved our asses." Hunter looked at his little sister and gave her a smile. "I don't know how long I could've held them off by myself, but she took care of them like *that*." He snapped his fingers in the air.

"Who was it?" Max asked. They'd reached the city limits again, and he sped up. He wasn't going nearly as fast as he had been on their way into town, but there was no need. "Do you have any idea who attacked you or why?"

Ava's eyes met Sarah's. "It was some of the younger Greystones. I recognized them. They didn't live at the packhouse, so I didn't know their names, but I'd seen them before when we were cleaning up after meetings."

Max nodded. "We'll get all this information to Rex. He needs to know. It was bold of them to go for you in public like that, but it's interesting that they didn't come to the house. I have to wonder what their strategy is. I'm glad you're safe, though. No injuries at all?"

Both of them said no, and the conversation seemed to be at an end for the moment. None of it was sitting well with Sarah, though. Everyone else thought things were fine, but they didn't feel the deep uneasiness that had settled over her shoulders.

Ava had used her magic. It'd saved both of their asses, and it would give them something to talk about for the rest of their lives. What they didn't understand was that Ava had used that magic right in front of two Greystones. They'd undoubtedly take that information right back to their pack. Edward had already made his feelings plain when it came to having witches in his bloodline, and now he'd have the proof that Ava was exactly the abomination he was trying to prevent.

11

MAX ROLLED HIS SHOULDERS UNDER THE HOT WATER, letting the jets pummel away at his muscles. Guards had been increased around the packhouse. Hunter and Ava had been thoroughly lectured about leaving the property without discussing it first, something they seemed to accept now. In fact, Rex had recommended that even the seasoned adults should exercise the greatest amount of caution possible. Rex had sent a message to Edward, suggesting that the two of them get together on neutral territory to discuss pack issues, but not admitting Sarah and Ava were being kept under Glenwood protection.

It was a start, and Max could feel that the tension of the other day had finally melted out of his body. He stepped out of the shower and wrapped a towel around his waist, studying his reflection as he ran a comb through his hair. Turning his head from one side to the other, he examined the flecks of silver in his stubble. He thought about shaving it off, but then remembered the way Sarah had run her fingers along his jawline. Granted, the two of them hadn't had a chance to be intimate again. Staying at the packhouse didn't make that particularly easy, nor did the fact that they'd been at each other's throats the day Hunter and Ava had gone into town.

Slicking on some moisturizer, Max reflected that in the moment, it'd felt like they might never come back from those arguments. He'd worried that Sarah didn't understand how much he sympathized with her and worried about her, and he might not have done a great job of explaining that. She was scared, and her fear could make her decide that Max and the Glenwoods wouldn't be enough to keep them safe.

Some of that fear, he knew, was boiling up from inside himself. He hadn't been able to protect her before, so how could he claim he could do it now?

Their argument, as frustrating and difficult as it'd been, hadn't resumed once they'd returned home. He could sense that Sarah's wolf still wasn't completely at ease, but he understood it wouldn't be for quite a while. At least the two of them were back to getting along on the surface. Max much preferred that to the opposite.

Still in a towel, he passed by her room on the way back from the bathroom and paused. He rapped his knuckles against the door.

"Come in."

He opened the door to find her in the chair by the French doors. Joan had tried to make Sarah's accommodations just as welcoming as Ava's. The chair had thick, soft upholstery and intricately carved wood around the edges, and it even had a matching footstool. Several decorative pillows had been arranged on the crisply made bed, and he spotted several new articles of clothing hanging in the closet.

Sarah looked fairly well at home as she looked up from her book, a sly smile creeping across her face as her eyes swept down his body. "I think you forgot something."

"Maybe I didn't." He enjoyed the way she drank him in with her eyes. It let him know she still wanted him just as badly as he wanted her. They might have their differences and were still getting used to each other again, but none of that could override their fate-bound connection. "We might be stuck here at the packhouse for a while, but nothing's saying we can't enjoy ourselves while we do."

Sarah pressed a hand to her collarbone. "Why, Max! How could you even suggest such a thing? It's not even dark outside yet."

He glanced out the French doors to the deck, where the afternoon sun was still shining brightly. "That just means I'll have an hour or so of sunlight to enjoy those curves before I take Ava and Hunter out for a run."

Sarah snapped the cover of her book shut. Her back stiffened, and any trace of humor had left her face. "Out for a run?"

Shit. So much for taking advantage of his lack of clothing. "I thought it'd be a good chance for Ava to work on her wolf again."

Her mouth was tight. "I don't think that's necessary right now."

"It is," he insisted, trying to make sure he kept the exasperation out of his voice. They'd already had such a hard time staying on even ground. He knew he was right and that this was right for Ava. "Her wolf is an important part of her. She's been spending a lot of time with Mom and Dawn while she works on her magic, and I think that's great. But she's struggled with shifting and needs to overcome this hurdle. She needs to know she can do this."

"So work on it in the yard. Hell, she's not very big. You can probably do it in the living room without even breaking a lamp. There's no reason she should have to go running off in the woods." Her knuckles turned white where she gripped her book.

"I have to disagree." The panic in her voice reflected the panic that was now blooming in his chest, though he had a feeling they were spurred by different things. Sarah worried for her children's safety. Max understood that, but another concern needed to be addressed sooner than later. "The only time Ava has been able to feel safe and carefree is while she's here in the packhouse. I'm grateful that we can give her that experience, but what kind of life will she live if she thinks something bad will happen to her every time she steps out the door?"

She flicked her eyes up at him. "I know what you're doing. You're trying to compare this to our confinement, but it's not the same, Max."

"No, but how long do we wait before she gets a chance at this life that you were fighting so hard for her to have?" he asked gently.

"You just don't understand." Sarah turned toward the window.

"That's what you keep telling me, but I really am trying." How could he get her to see it? "I'm just doing everything I can as a father to make sure something like what the kids just went through doesn't happen again. Eventually, Ava will move on and make her own life. She'll never be able to do that if she doesn't think she can leave her room. She needs to be able to shift and defend herself. The sooner she can get into training, the better."

"I don't want her to *train*," Sarah said firmly. "She's already had to fight too much in her short life. She shouldn't have to continue."

He tried to put himself in her shoes and see things her way, but he just couldn't. He could only come to the same conclusion that Ava needed to know what her body was capable of. It didn't matter that she was young or had never experienced her wolf before. She needed to know she could defend herself and protect her loved ones. Then there was the other reason this was so important. "She wants to train, Sarah."

Sarah closed her eyes, and her shoulders slumped forward.

"Brody and Hunter are coming with us," he pressed on, knowing it hurt her. Sarah didn't want to hear any of this. She didn't want her daughter to need protection from herself or anyone else. But the world didn't work that way. Even if the Greystones weren't after them, someone else would be at some point. It was exactly why the Glenwoods all learned basic fighting skills at a minimum. They didn't want to be caught unaware, assuming the world was a safe place. "I've already told you about how Rex has beefed up the number of guards posted at any given time, and that's not just here at the house. They're out on the property as well, serving as lookouts. I promise it'll be safe. We'll be back in a bit."

He felt like a complete asshole as he walked out of her room and back into his own to get dressed. He tossed on some joggers and a t-shirt. His wolf was irritated with him for leaving Sarah in her room. It longed to be with her, to feel her wolf and experience all the joy and comfort that was supposed to come from one's mate. He shoved it back down as he yanked on his shoes and tried to remind himself that even though things were hard right now, they wouldn't always be. Sarah would come around. He'd help Ava find her wolf, and then he'd get her into training. The girl would be so much more confident once she felt she could not only be one of the pack, but help defend it. Then everything would be okay.

He hoped.

"There you are," Hunter said as Max descended the stairs. "I thought maybe you'd forgotten."

"I didn't forget. I didn't even tell you a certain time, so there's no need to act like I'm late." Hunter and Ava looked like they were about to start bouncing off the walls.

"You could say they're a bit eager." Brody sat on the end of the sofa, his head bent and tipped as he scribbled on a small sketchpad. The Glenwood pack's new third in command was always drawing, something he'd been doing ever since he was a child. He'd managed to make it into a career as a tattoo artist, but even the art he got paid to do apparently wasn't enough to satisfy his creative needs. "They haven't stopped talking about it."

"I'm just excited." Ava grinned and looked toward the stairs. "Is Mom coming?"

Max hesitated. He didn't want to see the inevitable disappointment on Ava's face if she found out how Sarah felt about all this. She was smart and probably knew anyway, but Max wasn't sure he could break her heart like that. "She's going to stay here this time, but she said to have fun."

"Okay. So can we go?" Ava popped up on her toes and bounced, full of energy.

Well, his excuse had certainly rolled off her back,

but now Max felt guilty for lying to her. He'd have to get that settled later. Ava might be more capable of handling the truth once she'd learned to be comfortable in both her skin and fur. "Yeah, let's go."

When they reached the back of the yard, Max purposely led them off to the left so they'd take a different path than the one they'd been on the first time they'd tried. There was no guarantee that Ava would successfully shift, and he didn't want one certain section of the territory to make her feel like a failure.

Brody stepped up the front. He turned around and walked backward so he could see Max. "I think Hunter and I are going to go on ahead if you're good with that."

Max nodded. Brody had spent an awful lot of his free time training the young wolves. While none of them had ever been quite like Ava, Max trusted Brody's ideas. He knew, without even being able to speak telepathically at the moment, that Brody was trying to keep Ava from feeling like she had too much of an audience. "Sounds good. We'll meet you up near the waterfall."

Brody and Hunter turned and ran up the path, throwing themselves forward into their wolf forms as they did.

Ava sighed as she stared after them. "I can't wait to be able to do that."

"You will, honey." He said it as an encouragement, but Max also knew he meant it. He'd known Ava for such a short time, yet he could already see what a bright, determined young woman she was. "I know it sounds like this big, difficult thing right now, but it won't always be. You told me earlier that you were working on your shifting. What have you been able to do so far?"

"Not much," she admitted with a sheepish smile. "I keep trying, but I usually can't do more than a little here or there."

Though Max knew they weren't, it felt like the two of them were completely alone. Hunter and Brody were up ahead, and several other Glenwoods were spread throughout the woods, walking the paths, watching and listening. Still, as far as Ava was concerned, no one was there to judge her. "Can you show me?"

"Well, okay. But it's not very good." Ava flicked her hair back and shook out her arms to loosen them. She was doing just as he'd asked her to do when they'd gone out before, breathing deeply and trying to relax. A twinge of pain moved over her face as a stripe of fur slowly emerged on her forearm.

"Awesome job," he encouraged calmly. Inside, he was jumping for joy. It was small, but it showed she was adamant about making this happen. "That's a nice start. Anything else?"

Ava bent her arm across her stomach and held it in her other hand while the fur retreated. "Hunter and I have been talking about it a lot, and he's been trying to tell me what it's like. He thought maybe I could guide myself through it mentally, kind of like imagining that I really was doing it, and it might help."

Max would have to talk to the boy later. That was an impressive observation for such a young man. He was proud of Hunter both for thinking of it and being so genuine about wanting to help his sister. "Do you think it's helped so far?"

"Yeah. I mean, I couldn't do the thing with the fur before. I was just able to keep doing what you'd already seen me do with my claws." She tapped her nails against her thumb.

"Why don't you see if you can do them at the same time," he suggested. "Maybe you just need to start adding up small pieces at a time."

"I don't know." Ava's brows puckered, making a mirror image of the concern he'd seen on Sarah's face back at the packhouse.

His heart went out to his mate, even though she was probably pissed at him right now. This wasn't how he wanted any of this to be. He'd change it all if he could. He would've followed Sarah out of the house on that fateful night. They would've fought, yes, but they would've ended up coming back home. Then they'd raise their children together, and he would've taught his little girl to shift a long time ago. It would all have been so different, so less stressful, and he had to wonder how Selene could've let anyone be so tortured. Max pulled himself back into the moment, wanting to be there for Ava. "Just give it a shot. It's good practice no matter what happens."

"All right."

They were still walking, and Max didn't suggest that they stop. It looked impressive when someone shifted while on the move, but he knew sometimes it was actually easier than being at a standstill.

Once again, Ava tried to make herself relax. Someday, her wolf would come exploding out of her because of anger or some other strong emotion, but right now, her human was holding it back too tightly. Maybe the silver collar she'd been forced to wear her entire life was responsible for that. She let out a breath and tipped her head back. Nothing happened for a moment, but then he saw the stripe of fur appear on her arm. Good, that was a start. He watched her hand for the claws, but they didn't extend.

Max was just about to talk her through more techniques when he saw another stripe of fur erupt on her other arm. Then came the claws on one hand, making her cry out in pain, and then on the other hand. Ava stumbled to a halt. Her body convulsed as her bones twisted and changed. Max could feel her pain just as much as he could see it. He hated to watch her go through it, but he knew it was the only way.

"You're doing great. Just keep going. Let it come on out," he encouraged, wishing he could take the pain for his baby girl. "You're almost there, sweetie."

She let out one last strangled cry before she fell forward onto all fours. Max caught her before she hit the ground completely, holding her up as her tail appeared and her ears sharpened to a point. The golden eyes that looked into his were terrified.

He quickly let go of his human form, knowing he couldn't help her from two feet right now. *You did it, Ava!*

It feels so weird! She bent her head and stared at her paws. *I'm not sure if I like it.*

You're just not used to it, he assured her. *Try walking forward a bit.*

She moved her back feet, then realized she'd have to move the front ones to get them out of the way. Ava tried one set and then the other, hopping like a rabbit more than walking like a wolf.

It'll feel natural soon enough. I promise. Max moved alongside her, suddenly thinking a lot more about the cadence of his own steps, far more than he ever had before. *There you go.*

Wow. She picked her head up as her feet started to move more naturally. Her tail swished a little behind her, and her golden eyes lit up with excitement. *This is wild!*

He had to agree. Hunter had been so small when he'd learned to shift, just a chubby little pup. It was completely different with Ava, but no less special. *Why don't we pick up the pace and go find Hunter and Brody.*

Let's do it. It took her several starts and stops, and she stumbled over her feet a few more times, but they were soon loping up the hill toward the waterfall.

12

"HONEY, DIDN'T WE BRING MY FAVORITE SPATULA?" Brody called out as he dug around inside a canvas tote bag.

"I'm pretty sure I saw you put it in there." Robin shook her head and looked at Sarah. "The man is absolutely wild about his kitchen utensils."

"Don't shame me for being a man who enjoys high-quality kitchenware," Brody chided. "You've even said yourself how much nicer it is to use than the cheap stuff. Even Miss Evelyn here prefers to bang on pots and pans with superior utensils." He looked up from the tote to drop a kiss on his daughter's forehead.

"I'll help you look. Can you hold her for a sec?" Robin turned her hip toward Sarah.

Surprise took over her, but she quickly recovered and held out her hands. "Do you want to come to me?"

Evelyn regarded her with hazel eyes for a second before she launched herself out of Robin's arms. Sarah quickly grabbed her, wrapping her arms around Evelyn and bracing her against her hip. "You're a darling little thing, aren't you?"

"She doesn't know any strangers," Robin agreed as she triumphantly pulled Brody's favorite spatula out of the tote and handed it to him. "Every time I go to the store, she's waving at every person that walks by."

"It's not like it bothers anyone." Lori was at the sink, rinsing out a rag and getting the counters wiped down before Brody started cooking. "They ooh and aah over her and tell you what a doll she is. Believe it or not, strangers used to do that over my Conner at one point. As a college football player, he doesn't really have that effect on people now."

Robin and Lori laughed, but Sarah was completely entranced by Evelyn. She hadn't held a baby since Ava had been one. In some ways, that felt like yesterday. In others, it felt like a different lifetime. She sat in one of the kitchen chairs and moved Evelyn to her lap, supporting her around the ribs and letting the little girl play with strands of her hair. How had her own children grown so fast?

What pained her even more was knowing she'd missed almost all of it. Hunter walked into the kitchen just then, proving her point to herself. He'd been just about Evelyn's size when Sarah had been captured. Now he was practically a grown man, one who would soon start college and live his life for himself. He would never need her to wipe off his face or help him make sure he didn't put his shirt on backward. He'd probably already been through his first crushes and heartbreaks. What could she do about any of it?

"Hunter, perfect timing," Brody said when he saw his nephew. "I've got to get the noodles and the sauce going. I need you to chop some vegetables for me."

Hunter's lips pouted out. "Um, how do I do that?"

"Well, you can start by grabbing that red bell pepper and washing it," Brody suggested.

Lori was finished with the counter, and Sarah let her take the baby. There was a lot she wouldn't be able to do for her son, but at least she didn't have to feel completely useless. "I'll show you."

Hunter brought the pepper over to the cutting

board, looking at it like a foreign object. "Do I just chop it up?"

"Well, some ways are better than others," she explained. She'd taught Ava these sorts of things before, but they'd started out much younger so Sarah could keep her daughter with her when she had to work in the Greystone kitchen. "Start by turning it upside down, then make angled cuts like this. Then you avoid all the seeds and the stem."

"Oh, cool." Hunter took the knife from her and imitated her cuts. They were a little rough, but he got the job done.

"Then you can cut these pieces into strips and chop them up." Sarah quickly demonstrated what she meant.

"I never thought about this before," Hunter murmured as he focused hard on the rest of the pepper.

"You'll get another chance because I need some zucchini and an onion, too," Brody told him.

With the red pepper chopped and in a bowl, Hunter grabbed an onion and placed it squarely on the cutting board. "Same thing?"

"No, actually. Not at all." Sarah showed him how she chopped off each of the ends, which made it much easier to peel the skin off. "Then we can cut it in half, and chop each half into the small pieces that Brody needs." It was a small thing, but it made Sarah feel infinitely better. Hunter was learning something from her. He wasn't just tolerating her because she was his biological mother, nor was he trying to act like she had nothing to teach him.

"Like this?" He was slow and awkward, but he was getting the job done.

"Yep. Use your other hand to hold all those slices together so you can do them all at once when you come back the other way." She had to wonder what it'd been like to teach him other basic life skills as he'd grown up. Had he insisted on putting his shoes on the wrong feet? Had he thrown a fit when he couldn't get his coat off but refused help? Had he suddenly taken to cleaning his room and wanting it neat and tidy after years of leaving it messy? They were the tiniest of details, but right now, they felt so important to her.

"Something smells good," Ava announced as she came into the room, beaming from ear to ear. In fact, she'd been doing just that since she'd returned from her run.

"Only the best for the wolf of the hour!" Brody said with a grin.

Ava shook her head. "You don't have to make a fuss over me."

"Of course we do," Brody insisted. "Besides, I've already finely grated all the cheese by hand, so I can't turn back now. You just wait until you try this chicken Alfredo. It's like nothing you've ever tasted before."

Sarah's heart twisted with conflict. She didn't want Ava to be in any sort of danger, yet she couldn't help but be happy that her daughter had finally met the wolf that'd been trapped inside her for so long. She reached out to pull Ava into a half hug. "How are you doing today, sweetie?"

Ava gave her mother a confused look. "I'm fine, why?"

"I just worried that finally shifting might've worn you out a little," Sarah replied gently. She studied her daughter closely, but didn't see any signs of fatigue that she'd expected. Ava was bright and radiant, clearly still thrilled with what she'd been able to accomplish.

"Nope," her daughter confirmed with a little bounce. "I'm perfectly fine. Actually, I was thinking about asking to go out again sometime soon. I mean, I know I'm not ready to start training with the others yet, but—"

"Sure you are." Max appeared on the other side of the breakfast bar. He and Rex were both carrying in platters of meat from the smoker, filling the room with the most delectable scent. "You might not be able to keep up, but it's not like we'd ever leave anyone behind. It'd give you a chance to spend more time in your wolf with the others around, and that's an experience all in itself."

"I'm also a thorough believer in the idea that watching other people do something is one big step toward doing it yourself," Brody added from over by the stove. "Although right now, Max, I'd like to watch you bring me that chicken so I can get it sliced up and put in this dish."

"Yes, chef." Max obediently put the tray of chicken down by his brother and turned back to Ava. "I really do think it'd be fine. What do you think, Sarah?"

She was startled for the second time that evening when that question was directed at her. Ava's shifting success had made Sarah wonder if she'd been wrong. She hadn't wanted Max to take them out where there might be any chance of danger. It turned out he'd been completely right, though. Ava and Hunter were both fine, and Ava had made a huge breakthrough. What he proposed now would mean Ava would be surrounded by at least a dozen other Glenwoods. She wanted to trust Max, and she wanted to trust that they were safe. "Sure."

"Holy shit!" Hunter put the knife down and swiped his arm across his eyes. "I'd always heard that onions made people cry, but I thought that was just something they said on TV!"

Sarah laughed and handed him a paper towel. "I guess I should've told you to keep your head back so you wouldn't be right above it. I'll finish this."

As she chopped the onion and showed Hunter how to prep a zucchini, Sarah took a moment to notice everything happening around her. Joan and Jimmy were preparing drinks. Brody was doing the majority of the cooking, but everyone was helping, whether that meant handing him ingredients, washing dishes, or stirring the sauce while he did something else. Rex and Max had spent all afternoon smoking the meat. They didn't just leave one or two people to feed the whole pack, slaving away in the kitchen. It was like a real family. Until then, she didn't realize how badly she'd wanted one. Yes, she'd always wanted a mate and children, but this was bigger. This was incredible.

Her eyes lifted as Max came in from the garage, where he'd just taken out the trash. His face was soft and relaxed. He looked so different depending on his mood, but right now, he was obviously in a good one. She liked that, and she wanted to see more of it. She'd love to find more of it in herself. She'd have to remember that before she got angry and defensive next time.

The front door slammed. "Mom!"

"Conner!" Lori called back. "You're just in time. We were about to sit down and celebrate Ava's first shift. Come on in."

The big blonde linebacker grinned as he strode into the kitchen, his thick fingers clinging to those of a slim young woman about his age. Sarah remembered McKenzie from ages ago, but she'd just been a little girl back then. Now she stood next to Conner, looking up at him with sweetness in her eyes.

"I heard about that." Conner wrapped his free arm around Ava's shoulders. "Congrats! Do you mind if I butt in on your celebration with a bit of an announcement of my own?"

"Of course not." Ava looked so thrilled to be recognized by Conner. Sarah supposed he was like yet another big brother to her, especially since he and Hunter were so close.

Conner looked down at McKenzie and then lifted his head proudly as the rest of the Glenwoods turned to look at him. "McKenzie has officially accepted me as her mate."

"How could I refuse?" she giggled as she tipped her head to the side to show off the fresh bite mark in the curve between her shoulder and her neck.

"Conner! McKenzie! That's the best news I've ever heard!" Lori pushed her way toward her son so she could wrap them both in her arms. "I just knew it! I knew the two of you were meant to be. I could see it in your eyes."

Conner's face flushed with embarrassment but also pride.

"May Selene smile down on you both." Though Conner wasn't Joan's biological grandson, she still treated him as such. She kissed him and McKenzie on both cheeks.

Sarah watched the surge of awe and excitement over the young couple, gladly stepping aside so others could offer their congratulations. A faint buzzing rang in her ears as she watched Ava, who kept staring at McKenzie's shoulder.

"Plenty to celebrate, and plenty of food to do it with!" Brody announced as he held a huge bowl high over his head and led the way into the dining room, which could accommodate far more people than the kitchen table.

Everyone else followed, and Sarah soon found herself seated next to Max. Ava and Hunter were directly across from them, and there was constant chatter as everyone loaded their plates. The smoked meat made Sarah's mouth water. Brody had created a delectable chicken Alfredo, but there was also a huge salad, roasted vegetables, homemade rolls, herbed potato salad, and several other dishes that Sarah couldn't even fit on her plate.

"Butter?" Max asked as he handed her the dish.

Her finger grazed his as she took it, and she felt her wolf relax a little. It was a reminder that she needed to chill out a bit. She didn't always agree with the way things were done there, but she wasn't the one in charge. She was an outsider amongst the Glenwoods, despite the fact that they were protecting and caring for her. Everything would work out, and she'd get a chance to talk to Ava about a few things later.

"What are your plans for taking care of this young lady?" Rex was addressing his stepson several chairs down.

Conner had hardly taken his eyes off McKenzie, but neither had anyone else. "Well, we've got to finish college before anything else really happens. We thought we'd stay here and then get a place on our own after I graduate. If that's all right." His pride slipped a little, his cheeks reddening slightly.

Rex looked at him solemnly before his lips split into a grin. "Of course. I'd much rather you stay here and finish your education before you have to worry about putting a roof over your head."

"Man." Hunter had been watching them interact and turned back toward his plate, stabbing a big forkful of broccoli. "I can't wait to be lucky enough to find my mate one day and join the club."

"You have plenty of time," Max reminded him. "It happens when it's supposed to, so don't worry about it too much."

"I know, but there's no telling if it'll happen while I'm young like Conner or when I'm older like Brody and Rex were," Hunter replied. He frowned down at his plate for a second and then looked up at Sarah. "How old were you when you were marked?"

Sarah's teeth clamped together. It was suddenly far too hot in the room, and she was sure everyone was looking at her. The continual chatter of voices and clanging of silverware told her otherwise. Even if the whole table wasn't staring, her two children certainly were. Sarah turned to Max. He raised his brows and turned the corners of his mouth slightly down. He wasn't going to explain it to them. It had always been about her in the first place, and it still was. "I was never marked, actually."

Hunter's eyes remained glued on her, wide with disbelief. "You weren't? Dad, why didn't you—"

"I think this is something to discuss another time," Sarah cut in. It wasn't Max's fault, and in fact, Sarah didn't think there was really any fault to be had.

"But—"

"You heard what she said." Max swirled some noodles on his fork and stuffed them in his mouth.

Sarah decided it was also best to concentrate on her meal. She and Max had argued enough since she'd come back, and she sure as hell didn't want to start another one right there in front of the Glenwoods. That one little phrase he'd just uttered, however, told her that he had her back. No one ever said that raising children was going to be easy. The challenges were different when they were younger, but now she had to face the challenge of trying to explain herself.

It could wait, and the longer, the better.

13

"Hey, kiddo, how did you—" Max paused as he peeked into the living room. He'd wanted to see if Ava had enjoyed her celebration dinner, the first big event she'd attended with the Glenwood pack. He'd already been so proud of her for finally getting a chance to experience her wolf, and it deepened his joy to know that the pack was happy to share in honoring the day.

But Ava was busy. She was standing near the fireplace, raptly listening as Dawn and Joan explained something to her. Max couldn't quite hear what it was, but he had an inkling. His sister and mother had been thrilled to find that the witch bloodline had continued on, and they'd taken Ava under their wing. He didn't want to interrupt, so he stepped back into the kitchen.

Sarah had her back to him while she stood at the sink, washing the last dishes that wouldn't fit in the dishwasher. Max watched her for a minute, admiring the swell of her hip under her jeans and the way her hair trailed across the dark blue of her shirt. She flicked her head slightly to the side, exposing that gentle curve between her neck and shoulder that had gone unmarked as of yet.

Pain pricked inside his gums as his fangs threatened to descend, and he quickly worked to keep his wolf at bay. That was an argument he'd let go of a long time ago, though he'd never been satisfied with it. He and Sarah had different viewpoints on the tradition, and he'd tried to tell himself that it wasn't a big deal. It had only mattered that they were together. Now they had other eyes watching them besides the adults in the pack. They had children to raise. Hunter might be a man by legal standards, but he wasn't done growing and learning just yet.

The one thing he could take comfort in was that the subject had been dropped, and dinner had carried on with a toast both to Ava and the newly-mated couple. Max had sensed how uneasy Sarah had become when Hunter asked about her mark, but she hadn't reacted the same way she had to everything else that was difficult for her. Maybe they were making progress.

He stepped up behind her, resting his hands on her hips. Her scent drifted up to him, a lavish mix of flowers. He didn't know the scents well enough to parse them all out, but she smelled like the warm riot of blooms that emerged every spring. His wolf sensed her proximity, and he pressed himself against her back. Hell, he couldn't fool himself. It wouldn't matter if they were arguing or not. He'd still want her. "Those dishes are getting an awful lot of attention."

"I think they deserve it after feeding so many hungry wolves." She turned just slightly so that he could see the profile of her face. "I take it they're not the only ones who need attention."

His heart rate picked up as he studied that forbidden skin. It would be so easy to let his fangs descend and—no. That wasn't how it was done. "I might."

She rinsed off her hands and turned in his arms. "I didn't know you were into hot, soapy water."

His blood throbbed through his body and went

straight to his groin. It would be so easy to slip upstairs and into the spacious shower. Soap was just a means to get clean, but not if Sarah was in there with him. He longed to see the lather all over her body, to feel it under his hands, to—

"Hey, Dad!" The garage door slammed behind Hunter as he came into the kitchen. "What are you guys doing tonight? I had some ideas about what I want to do after I graduate, and I wanted to see what you thought."

Max looked down at his mate. She was tempting. Not just tempting. Irresistible. With her there against him, it was hard to remind himself that he also had the responsibility of being a father. He bent down to her ear, her hair tickling his lips. "There's nothing I want more than to throw you over my shoulder and take you upstairs, but I guess that'll have to wait for later."

The tip of her tongue touched her teeth. "Promise?"

Did she know what she was doing to him? Probably, but he'd take the torture. Max turned to Hunter. "Sure. I think Ava's in the living room. Let's head in there."

The three of them stepped through to the front

room. Joan and Dawn had gone off somewhere else, but Ava lingered by the fireplace. The tiny flame that crackled inside illuminated her face, but not as much as her sheer joy when she turned around. "Hey!"

"Hi. Isn't it a little warm out for a fire?"

A flicker of uncertainty crossed her face. "I made it." She wiggled her fingers.

Max suddenly understood. She'd been working with the other two witches in the house, and just like that, there was a fire in the fireplace. Ava hadn't made this fire by striking a match or even using a flint. She'd used her magic. "That's amazing!"

"We don't have to keep it going, though." Ava reached for the rack of fireplace tools, intending to grab the shovel and smother the flame with ash.

"Sure, we do." Max put his hand out to stop her. "It's an accomplishment, and we'll enjoy it." He moved to sit on the loveseat.

Sarah sat down next to him, and he easily draped his arm over her shoulders as the kids settled in across from them. Max pulled in a breath and checked in with his wolf, feeling instantly how satisfied it was. It took a long time to get there, but this is how things were always supposed to be. His younger self had been caught up in the thrill of a woman that belonged only to him, and he to her. Max still felt that way, but there was so much more to it than that. They'd had some rough patches, and in the back of his mind, he knew they weren't completely smoothed over yet, but this was the stuff dreams were made of. He relaxed into the back of the sofa.

"Okay." Hunter was sitting in an upholstered chair, but he was so excited, he was barely putting his weight on it. He leaned forward, his elbows on his knees. "I thought about going to college with Conner."

"You'd mentioned that before." Max liked the idea. It'd give Hunter a certain sense of freedom and independence, but he'd also have his family and pack close by when he needed to lean on them.

Sarah beamed at her son. She'd missed so much while he was growing up, but Max could see just how eager she was to take part in any way she could. "Have you thought about what you might want to major in?"

"At first, I was thinking about environmental studies. It made sense, considering where we live and how important the land is to the pack," Hunter explained. "I'm starting to get a few other ideas, though."

Max smiled. "Like what?"

"Like not going to college at all."

Max cleared his throat and shifted slightly in his seat. Deciding on a major sounded like a pretty easy conversation, but now it was taking a much more complicated turn. "I thought that was what you wanted."

"I'm not sure if I really do or if I was just trying to make everyone else happy. Taking a gap year is starting to sound like a good idea. I could travel the world, see all sorts of things, and meet new people. It could be awesome." Hunter slapped his hands on his knees.

Sarah pressed her tongue against the inside of her cheek. "It's an interesting idea."

"Or, I thought I might join the military," Hunter continued. "It'd just be a different way of traveling the world, plus I wouldn't have to pay for it."

Max liked to think of himself as a pretty liberal parent. He knew he couldn't tell Hunter what to do anymore, but a heavy ball of dread settled in his stomach. "Hunter, it's honorable to serve your country. You'd undoubtedly get an education, whether in life, or if you went to school afterward. But you have to consider the fact that most people in the service aren't like us. You could get hurt, and it's unlikely that you'd see a doctor who understands shifter anatomy. You could be exposed."

"I *could* be, but it won't necessarily happen," Hunter reasoned. "I'd just have to be careful. Other shifters have done it. Just think of the veterans who formed those Special Ops Shifters units around the country. I could be one of them someday! How cool would that be?"

"Yes, but—"

"It's a great idea," he insisted. "Ava thinks so, too. Right, Ava?"

She'd been staring into the fireplace, fiddling with her necklace, and now she looked up dreamily. "What's up?"

Sarah laughed. "Where have you been? You haven't heard a word?"

Ava's beatific smile widened. She got up from her chair and padded over, bending down to show her mother the pendant she wore. "Grandma Joan just gave this to me. She said it's been in her family for a long time."

Sarah touched the iridescent stone set into gold. "It's very pretty. That was nice of her."

"She wasn't just being nice," Ava clarified. "It's a moonstone. She said it'll provide protection and blessings from Selene. I didn't know who that was, but she told me all about the moon goddess and how she helps people like me."

"Take it off." Sarah's voice was thick with anger. "Take that off right now."

Ava clutched her hand around the pendant and took a step back. "But Grandma Joan gave it to me. I like it."

Max pulled his arm out from around Sarah's shoulders so he could turn toward her. "Maybe this is something we should talk about later."

"No, I think we've had about enough of that." Sarah shot up off the couch and held out her hand. "Take it off and give it to me."

"Mom!" Ava's eyes welled as she backed up again, looking at Hunter and Max. Her cheeks reddened. "You're embarrassing me!"

"There are things much more important than being embarrassed!" Sarah flung out her hand to emphasize what she'd already asked her daughter to do. "I don't want you to have anything to do with Selene."

Ava's hands shook as she undid the clasp and dropped the necklace in Sarah's palm. "I can't believe you would do this to me!"

"You'll understand when you're older."

But Ava didn't stick around to hear anything that

Sarah had to say. She darted from the room, sobs escaping her lips as she hurtled up the stairs. Her bedroom door slammed shut a moment later.

A thick silence descended on the living room. The fantasy of a happy little family had been utterly destroyed, all over a simple necklace. Max steeled his jaw. He knew what was coming, and he was ready for it. He pulled in a breath, ready to tell Hunter to leave the room. What he had to say to Sarah probably shouldn't be said in front of their son, even if he was eighteen.

"I can't believe your mother would do that," Sarah snapped before Max had a chance to get the first word out.

"Excuse me?" Max had understood a long time ago that Sarah didn't agree with the way his pack did things, but this felt like a direct attack on his mother. He didn't like it.

Sarah put the necklace down on the coffee table and dusted off her fingers as though it'd left a nasty residue behind. "She knows—she *has* to know—how I feel about the whole Selene thing. But did that matter? No, she just waltzed right up and bestowed Ava with some family heirloom, all to make it seem so special and make sure that Ava couldn't say no. She should've asked me first."

"I'm sure she didn't mean anything by it," Hunter started.

"That's really not the point." Sarah folded her arms in front of her chest.

"But it *is* a point," Max countered. "Selene is important to this pack, even if not to you. You can't just pretend that she doesn't exist, and you don't get to decide everything for our kids."

"It seems like I don't get to decide much of anything." Rage filled Sarah's eyes as she turned to look at him. "The choice gets taken away from me almost every damn time there's one to be made. Everyone else always thinks they know best. Everyone else is always right. And what about me, Max? When do I get to have a say? Or do I have to bow my head and just go along the lines of tradition simply because that's what the pack demands? Trust me, I've had more than my fair share of listening to the pack." She turned in a hurry and left the room.

Max's wolf reacted violently, remembering that the argument on that fateful night so many years ago hadn't been so different. He'd dug in his heels and made all his points, but she'd dug in her heels and resisted all of them. At least this time, she went upstairs instead of outside.

When her door shut, Hunter turned to Max. "Maybe I can talk to her."

Max's heart went out to his son. He was just a kid, really, but he was trying so hard to be an adult. It made Max proud to know that he'd at least done a few things right. "I appreciate that, son, but this is between the two of us. There's no need for you to get involved."

"But she might listen to me," he insisted. "She's my mom, even if I haven't had her around all this time."

"She is, but this debate dates back to before you were even born. I'll handle it." Max put his hands on his hips and looked at the staircase. Half of him wished that Sarah would come back down and finish the fight. He wanted to tell her how angry he was for the way she'd hurt Ava. He wanted to yell and scream and let her know just how much she'd hurt him, too. But the other half of him knew that it probably wouldn't do any good.

"I'm going to go see what Conner is up to," Hunter mumbled as he headed off. "He's probably busy with McKenzie, though."

Max was left alone. He wondered if that was how he was going to end up permanently. He picked up the fireplace shovel and slowly doused the little flame that Ava had been so happy about. It was impossible not to see the connection between that fire and the family that had finally been brought back together. Both were the work of magic, and it seemed that both were too fragile. He'd hoped beyond hope that he and Sarah could manage to keep their little family together, but now he wasn't sure he could do it.

14

"WHAT CAN I GET FOR YOU?" MAX SHOUTED ABOVE
the bump and thrum of the music at Selene's. He
could hardly even pick up a rhythm from the band's
racket, but that was fine. The noise was just what he
needed, tunneling into his ears to drown out his
other thoughts.

"Bourbon. Neat."

"Coming right up." It was too simple. While Max
had never been a big fan of making mixed drinks in
the past, right now, he wanted something more than
just dumping a bit of bourbon in a rocks glass and
sliding it across the bar. "Here you go. How about
you?" He turned to the next customer.

"I just want a moment to talk to my brother."

Dawn gave him a finger wave and smiled. "I'll take a margarita, though."

"No wine tonight?" He knew all their regulars pretty well, but he definitely knew his sister.

She shrugged. "So I want something different. Let me live a little."

"Coming right up." It wasn't exactly complicated, but it would keep his hands busy for a moment. He grabbed a shaker and added tequila. "What brings you in? You usually go right home after working those long shifts."

The music came to a crashing stop. "Thank you, Eugene! We love playing here at Selene's. The Bed Bugs will be back again next week, so make sure you come on out and see us!" Recorded rock tracks started playing in the absence of the band, which were blessedly quieter than The Bed Bugs had been.

Dawn watched Max bypass the premade margarita mix and grab fresh lemons and limes. "Can you muddle a few jalapeño slices in there? And yeah, I do. I heard you were actually here tonight, though, and I thought maybe it was time we had a little chat."

"Hmph." Things were slowing down a little now that the live band had stopped playing. Max looked over and saw that Lori had stepped up to the bar, so she could handle any other patrons. He tossed some jalapeño slices into the shaker and muddled them with the tequila. "I guess I have a minute."

"I imagine you have more than a minute if you're actually working a full shift here. You've hardly left the packhouse at all since Sarah's been back." Dawn tipped her head to the side, watching him carefully.

After he'd added the remaining ingredients and poured the drink into a salted glass, Max firmly slid it across the bar. "Very observant," he replied carefully.

"So what's changed?" She picked up the glass by the stem and took a slow sip. "There isn't enough lime juice."

"Would you prefer to come back here and make it yourself, *Karen*? Or would you like to speak to my boss? I'm sure Rex would be more than happy to dump that free drink of yours down the drain." He shook his head. "I figured it was about time I came back to work. Rex has been understanding about all the time I've been taking off, but I'm still an employee here." He rinsed out the shaker and ran it through a sink of soapy water. Max sure as shit wasn't getting behind on the dishes tonight.

"He's your brother. He's not going to fire you," Dawn pointed out.

"Yeah, well. Maybe I needed a little time to get out of there. A man can't stay inside the same four walls—or even on the same acreage, before you correct me—for days at a time without getting a little stir crazy." Granted, the distraction of Selene's wasn't as much of a help as he'd anticipated. At least he didn't feel like he had to avoid Sarah every time he walked down the hallway. It even felt awkward to talk to Ava or Hunter, since they were caught in the middle.

"You could always go home. I mean, it makes sense for Sarah and Ava to stay at the packhouse, but it doesn't mean you have to." She took another sip. "No, it really does need more lime."

Max grabbed a lime slice from the bin and dropped it in her glass. "There. Good enough?"

Another customer stepped up to the bar, slipping between Dawn and the next barstool. "Hey, man. I need another beer, like pronto." Even though he was leaning on the bar, he managed to stumble into Dawn.

"Watch it," Max snapped. "You don't just walk up between people like that, you know. There's an open spot right down there."

"I'm so wasted, I can't see shit!" the punk said with a laugh, slapping the bar as though he'd just made the best joke ever. "Can you just get me my beer, man?"

"Hang on." Not even bothering to ask him what he wanted, Max pulled the cheapest draught they had and handed it over. "There."

"Thanks, man. You're the best."

"Right." Max watched him stagger off. Most people who came to Selene's behaved themselves. They were a rough crowd in a lot of ways, but there was a certain line that didn't get crossed. Max thought he might need to watch this one, or maybe he was just too pissy to be working behind a bar tonight.

"Anyway," Dawn said when they were relatively alone again. "I know there are problems between you and Sarah. I'm just worried about you."

"There's nothing to worry about." Max grabbed a rag and wiped down the bar, not liking the way her hazel eyes were on him.

"I beg to differ. It doesn't take a genius to see the tension between the two of you, Max. It might help to talk about it." She poked at her lime with a short, unpainted fingernail.

"Fine." He didn't really want to. Max had kept his guilt over Sarah to himself all these years, and he hated to just turn around and blab about his feelings, even to Dawn. He could handle it on his own. He didn't need any help. "If it'll make you happy."

"It will." Dawn whipped her head to the side as the same punk came up next to her, nudging her arm with his elbow as he did. "Geez, dude. I think you've had about enough to drink."

"I'm barely even buzzed," he replied, even though he'd just claimed a minute or so ago that he was drunk.

"What do you want?" Max growled. "I already gave you a beer."

"It was the wrong one. I wanted a stout. That's what real men drink." He turned back toward Dawn and leered at her. "That's what you'd like, right? A real man?"

"What I'd like is for you to get the fuck away from me." Dawn's mouth twisted up into a sneer.

"Just take this and go, okay?" Max handed him a stout, wondering just how much leeway Rex would give him if he got a little rough with one of the customers. He didn't want to put up with any more bullshit.

"Fine. But you don't know what you're missing, baby." The man gave Dawn a sloppy wink before heading back to his table.

"I can't even imagine what he might think if he

sobered up and realized I'm old enough to be his mother," Dawn said with a shake of her head. "Anyway, talk to me, Max. Let's get it all out before he comes back."

He pressed his hands into the bar, wishing the solid reality of it would ground him and make him feel as though he could make rational decisions about this. "I was beyond happy to find out that she was alive. I had her back, and I had a daughter, and I thought everything was going to be just fine."

"But it's not," Dawn concluded.

"No, not really. It was easy to forget the fights we used to have when we were younger, but they keep coming back up. There's a lot we don't agree on, especially when it comes to raising the kids." He slapped his hand on the bar and straightened up. "She just refuses to see my point of view. And I don't understand why she picks some things to be fine with and not others."

Dawn raised an eyebrow. "Like what?"

"Like she's completely fine with the fact that Ava is a witch, even though it was our bloodline that had made her father try to keep us apart. But then she's all weird about how we still follow Selene, and last night she tried to equate it to following along blindly with the pack."

"Hm."

"What does that mean?" he asked impatiently.

Setting down her margarita, Dawn leaned forward and crossed her arms on the bar. "Ava's magic is something she inherited. It's a part of her, and there's nothing anyone can do to make it go away. Same thing with her wolf. Selene, though, that's more of a choice."

"So what, you're siding with her now?" Max picked up the rag again but then dropped it. There wasn't a damn thing left to clean.

"No, I'm just making an observation." Those hazel eyes, the same ones their mother had, followed his every move.

"Then maybe you should go observe Sarah for a little while and figure out why she's being like this. Even if you're right about Selene, why is Sarah so adamantly against it? She tried to equate it to her own pack and Edward. I don't get it." He'd turned it over a dozen times in his mind, hardly able to sleep at all after their last fight, and he hadn't come to any conclusions.

Dawn, however, was nodding. "I think that makes sense, actually."

"Are you shitting me?"

"Not in the least. Max, it was the traditions of

Sarah's pack that kept the two of you from being together. They might, in general, be a more modern pack, but I'll bet she sees Edward's hate for witches as being the same thing as our love for Selene. It all boils down to doing what's expected of you simply because you're part of a pack. In her case, she probably feels like she has to go against the grain just so she has some control over her life," Dawn mused.

"I don't know about that." She had a bit of a point, but he wasn't really interested in it right now. "I think it's just because she's so damn stubborn, just like she's always been."

"Kind of like someone else I know." His sister smiled at him. "I guess you could say it takes one to know one."

Max let a breath out through his nose. "You're not helping. And you're not there when Sarah completely flips out over something that shouldn't be a big deal."

"To you," Dawn returned quickly. "She's been through a lot, Max."

"So have I." He grabbed the rag once again and slapped it down onto the bar. It didn't do much of anything to alleviate the sheer irritation that burned inside him. "I might have had my freedom technically, but I had to raise a son on my own when I thought my mate had been killed. It's not like I've been skipping through the grass all these years."

"Exactly, my dear brother." Dawn reached across the bar and grabbed his hand. "Did you ever think that perhaps the two of you are both so stubborn because you *needed* to be that way? You would've had an impossible time raising Hunter if you weren't so strong and determined. Sarah has to have those same qualities, or she would've given up a long time ago and never come back to you. I think you just need to look at it from a different perspective."

"There she is." The drunk came wobbling back over. One eyelid was sagging, and he bounced in place as he spoke to Dawn. "I just can't stop looking at you. I know there's something between us. You feel it, too, don't you?"

"Oh, not the same way you're about to," Dawn murmured. She swirled her finger in a downward spiral over the bar.

"Mmhmm." Clearly not picking up on her tone of voice or any other clues she'd given him, the man sidled closer. "You're a sweet thing, aren't you?"

Dawn grinned. "Not really."

"You've been lookin' at me all night." His head lolled from side to side. "What do you do, baby?"

"I'm a nurse."

Max couldn't figure out why she was even bothering to talk to him. "Dawn, let me just throw this guy out."

"First, as a medical professional, I need to let him know that drinking so much can have a serious impact on his digestive system," she replied with a slow smile. "It doesn't always come on right away, but it happens."

The drunk's eyes widened, and his shoulders stiffened. "I gotta go now."

"I know. Bye." She laughed as she watched him run to the bathroom, trying to rip his pants off before he even got through the door.

Max put it all together. "You did that to him, didn't you?"

She rolled a shoulder. "Drinking too much really can cause diarrhea. I can't really be blamed if I helped things along a little."

He'd been so angry and frustrated all day, but he couldn't help but laugh. "Rex should hire you as a bouncer."

"I'll pass. I deal with enough difficult people at the hospital, thank you very much. But back to the subject at hand, I think you need to find a way to talk to Sarah. Start trying to think about things from her perspective, and she'll probably do the same," Dawn advised.

Max opened his mouth to reply, but he shut it again. "There's just no good way to go about it. If I try to talk to her, it's going to start another argument, and then where will I be?"

"And where will you be if you don't talk to her at all?" Dawn pointed out. She tossed back the last spicy sip of her margarita. "I've got to get going, but at least think about it, okay? Sarah's a good person. She's having a hard time, and so are you, so none of this will be easy. If anyone can make it happen, though, it's you. Let me know how it goes." She slid off her stool and headed for the door.

Max sighed as he watched her go. It was something to think about, yes, but he wasn't convinced it would have the same results Dawn was hoping for.

15

SARAH LOOKED AT HERSELF IN THE MIRROR. SHE'D done it so many times since she'd come to stay at the Glenwood packhouse, but her reflection didn't give her any more solutions now than it had before. She felt tired, and she looked it. Her eyes drooped, and the corners of her mouth kept turning down. Sometimes spritzing her hair and giving it a quick shot with the blow dryer made her feel better, but it wasn't helping this time.

She wasn't sure anything would.

Her heart thudded when a knock came at her door. She knew it was Max before she even called out. Perhaps it was the way he knocked, but Sarah knew better. It was simply because it was him. That was all the information her wolf needed. "Come in."

He slowly opened the door and stepped inside. His dark hair was carefully combed, but he still had that sexy salt-and-pepper stubble that'd become part of his look. "Hey. Do you have a minute?"

Sarah rubbed her lips together. "I do, but I have a feeling this is going to take more than a minute."

Max let out a short, dry laugh. "Yeah, I guess it will. Sarah, we need to talk. And I know anything we have to say to each other will be difficult, but I'd like us to do everything we can not to turn it into another fight."

"I agree. I don't want to fight with you anymore, Max."

Footsteps crashed down the hall, and young male voices echoed with them. It was probably Hunter and Conner, or some of the other young wolves in the packhouse.

"Let's step outside," Max suggested.

Sarah slipped through the French doors onto the deck. The afternoon was a relatively cool one, considering the warm weather they'd been having, and she needed that breeze on the back of her neck to drive away the beads of sweat forming there. She wished it could also blow away the sense of impending doom that writhed within her, but it didn't. Sarah's wolf had been restless for the last couple of days, ever since the last 'discussion' she and Max had in the living room. The beast had been even more keyed up today, probably because it knew what was coming.

She rested her elbows on the railing and looked out over the yard. A faint breeze ruffled the trees. Several darker clouds had gathered in the distance and were moving in swiftly. Sarah welcomed the rain and storms they would likely bring because they'd match the feeling in her heart.

"Sarah, I'm sorry," Max began as he came to stand next to her. "I'm sorry for everything I said and did that made you feel like I didn't understand you. The truth is I don't think I *do* understand. I've been trying."

She nodded. "We've lived very different lives. Whenever I think we're back on the right track again, we get derailed. We've always known that we haven't completely agreed on everything, though."

"That's true." He let out a long breath, but it wasn't laced with a growl this time. He wasn't angry, at least. "I like to think we might've been able to work that out if we'd had the chance."

Her heart slowly sank to the bottom of her stomach, lying on its side and sloshing back and forth. She'd known it was coming. She'd planned on saying such things herself. So why did it feel so much worse to hear Max say it, too? "I've wondered about that myself. Maybe too much time has gone by, changing both of us in different ways. We're not young kids who still have their whole lives ahead of them, like Conner and McKenzie."

He rubbed the back of his neck. "I knew that you weren't into the whole Selene thing, but I didn't realize just how adamantly against it you were. I'm still not sure I understand why, but I didn't like seeing how upset Ava was."

She'd already put a knife through her own heart with that one, and now Max was twisting it. Sarah knew she deserved it, though. "I've spoken to her about it, and I've apologized. I wish I could've stayed calmer and addressed it differently, but I still feel the same about it."

"You know, I guess I always thought you'd just come around to it eventually. Back when we were younger, I mean. That wasn't very smart of me, but most young men aren't that smart to begin with. They're too busy thinking about other things to focus on the real stuff." He curled his fingers on the outside of the railing and leaned back. "It catches up with them eventually."

"There's more between us than just sex," she

corrected him gently. No matter what happened in this conversation, she wanted to make sure he knew that.

"Yes, but I'm starting to think it isn't enough." He closed his eyes. "I feel defeated."

"Funny how we can fight with each other and both come out the loser." Sarah felt that same sense of defeat down to her very bones. Her wolf despised it. It urged her to keep fighting until she found a better outcome, to do something about this already. But Sarah was tired. She'd fought for so long. How much longer would she have to keep going? How much longer *could* she keep going?

Max turned to her. "When you showed up at the door, I thought all my dreams had come true. I thought I was finally getting everything I wanted in life. I've had some of those same feelings again as we've been trying to work this out, but I'm starting to think we might have jumped into this too quickly. We just assumed we were the same kids who used to know each other, but maybe we're not."

Every part of her was shattering, splintering into a million pieces that could never be glued back together. She'd picked them up and carried them around, trying to look strong on the outside so Ava and Hunter wouldn't know the difference, but Sarah knew she'd never be whole again. "No. I don't think we are."

One corner of his mouth twitched up. "So this is when we finally start agreeing?"

"I guess so." She looked down at her hands. They were hardened and calloused from so many years of work, laboring away so others could have the lives they wanted. No amount of hard work would bring her the life *she* wanted, and the injustice of it sat bitterly within her. The problems between herself and Max had always been there, but she had no doubt they'd been compounded by their time apart. It was all because of Edward and his cruel, stubborn ways, and anger piled on top of her sadness. Why couldn't things have been different?

"I remember hearing my parents and other adults talking about how great it was to find your mate, that it made your life whole and everything better. They don't talk about all the complications that can come with it, though. It's been even tougher for us, and I think we've been too hard on ourselves by trying to force it," Max said quietly.

Tears threatened, but she held them back. They could come later when she had time to let them all out. "Hunter and Ava are almost grown, but they still need us. We can take some time to be apart, though.

Ava and I will stay here for a little while, but when we're sure it's safe, we'll get our own place. I'll find a job, and I'll get her enrolled in school. She can go to your place to see you and Hunter, and she can come here to visit with the rest of the pack. I'm sure she'll want to continue her magic training with Joan and Dawn." It was practical. It was right. It would save them all a lot of heartache, and it would provide a more stable environment for the kids. So why did it hurt so much?

"Thank you." Max took a step back, but he still lingered. "There's always a chance we might work it out in the future, right?"

Her tongue longed to tell him yes, that they just needed some time and space. Her heart wasn't entirely sure. "I think I'm still trying to figure out who I am, Max. I've been living my life for other people for almost my entire adulthood. I don't really have a clue what I like or what I want. I don't even know what I like to read or watch on television. The world has changed without me, and I have a lot of catching up to do."

"It'll be—" Max's spine had stiffened, and his eyes peered out into the trees. "Do you see that?"

The wind was a little heavier now as the storm crept closer. Sarah scanned the yard, her lupine defenses immediately on alert. There was too much movement, and her eyes were trying to take it in. "What?"

"I swore I just saw someone down there, near the cedar tree."

Her heart was out of her stomach now, but she could feel it throbbing in the back of her throat. Her wolf pushed up toward the surface, ready to emerge. She'd been trying all day to search for the practical answers and the calm way of doing things, but it wasn't easy right now. "Could it just be Conner or someone else?"

"Possibly." His voice was full of doubt, and she felt it inside her. "There."

Sarah looked where Max pointed. A man stepped out of the woods. He was far enough away that he couldn't be seen all too easily, but she recognized his stance. "I know him. That's Carter, one of Edward's guards."

"What about that one?" Max's gaze shifted to another part of the tree line near a cottonwood.

"Frank." He was slightly closer, and she could see the scar. "And Emory is just over there. Even Gina is here." The Greystones were appearing out of the woods, surrounding the house. Sarah could only see from this vantage point, but she knew how they operated. "They must be all around us by now."

"Find the kids and make sure they're safe. I'm getting Rex. Sarah. Sarah!"

She heard him talking, but his words weren't registering. The next figure that came lumbering out of the woods was one she recognized all too well. It was a man who had demanded more from her than any person could ever give, and he'd ruined her life in return. "Edward's here."

"I'm not surprised." Max grabbed her arm and pulled her toward the door. "Get Hunter and Ava, and alert anyone else you see on the way. We're in for a battle."

16

THE FIGHT HAD BEEN COMING FOR A LONG TIME. THE few moments of peace Sarah had bought herself by staying with the Glenwoods had been artificial, a nice distraction from the inevitable. The reckoning had come.

Sarah's body had obeyed Max's commands. She'd rounded up the children and checked every room, ensuring everyone knew what was happening. Ava now stood in the living room with her big brother's arm around her. Conner and McKenzie were there with them, along with Joan and Jimmy. Brody stood to the side, talking to Max. Robin had gone into the safe room in the basement with little Evelyn, as had a few other mothers with their young children. Lori and Dawn stood in the kitchen doorway, their backs turned to the rest as they watched the back of the packhouse. Guards had been stationed throughout the place and even on the rooftop as they waited. Sarah braced her hand on the corner of the wall, trying to figure out what to do with herself.

The knock on the door sent a shiver of fright down her body and into her very soul. Sarah couldn't go back. She'd managed to escape, and she couldn't imagine what it might be like to live that nightmare all over again.

Rex pushed through the crowd. "Everyone stay here and stay calm," he ordered. "Remember your training."

Sarah's breath was coming in ragged gasps now. She had no training. She had nothing to fight with but her teeth and claws, which wouldn't be enough. She'd never be able to take them down. When Rex opened the door, she saw a glimpse of her father. To her dismay, Rex stepped outside and closed the door behind him.

She rushed to Max. "Get him back inside! He's going to get killed out there!"

"He knows what he's doing." Jimmy patted her elbow.

"Glenwood, you're harboring two fugitives from

my pack," Edward's voice boomed through the open window.

"No, I'm not," Rex replied calmly.

This wasn't a simple social call, and Sarah's guts twisted at the idea of Rex being out there with them, Alpha or not.

"Don't bother with semantics," Edward warned. "Whether you want to call them fugitives or not, you know exactly who I'm speaking about. I'm here for Sarah and Ava."

"Well, you're not going to get them. They're under our protection."

Sarah closed her eyes. She had wanted that protection so badly, but at what price?

"I'm going to make this easy on you, Glenwood. People say I'm a hard man, but I'm actually very easy to get along with. Everyone in my pack would tell you so," Edward boasted.

"I'll bet."

Edward either didn't notice the humor in Rex's voice or chose to ignore it. "It's simple, really. You turn Sarah and Ava over to us, and we'll leave you in peace. If not, your pack will be destroyed."

The thought came to Sarah's mind so fully formed that she hardly mulled it over before stepping toward the front door.

A hard, muscular arm shot out to stop her. "What are you doing?"

She looked up at Max. He'd never understood her, not really. Not the way she wanted him to. It was even harder for him now, but she would make him. "I'm going out there. I'm going to give myself up to Edward."

Anger burned in his eyes. "Why would you do that?"

"Maybe I can convince him to take me and leave Ava alone. Then I'll never have to worry about her. She'll stay with you, Max. Where she'll be safe." She tried to take another step.

He moved fully in front of her now. "Are you out of your mind? I don't care what we just said upstairs. I'm not letting you do this."

"We don't have a choice." She couldn't keep the trembling out of her voice, but there was no time to be embarrassed about it now. This was her last chance to save Ava from Edward's clutches, and she was going to take it.

"I've got your place fully surrounded," Edward warned Rex. "It wouldn't take us more than a few minutes to end you all. I'm more than happy to add to the Greystone territory by taking over yours, if that's the way you want to do this."

She hated her father with the vilest hostility she could muster, and she hated him all the more for proving her point just now. "See? I have to go."

"Hell no, Sarah. He'll probably kill you before you're even off the property," Max growled. "It's not happening. We're here to protect you, and that's the end of it."

Desperation welled up inside her. They had all done so much for her, but there had to be a limit. "I can't have any Glenwoods hurt or killed for my sake."

A soft and gentle hand rested on her shoulder. "That's exactly what a pack should do," Joan said softly. "You might not have been born into the Glenwoods, Sarah, but you're one of us. Nothing is going to change that. Nothing," she added again when she saw that Sarah was about to argue with her.

The door opened, and Rex came back inside. All eyes were on him. "I spoke with their Alpha. He has certain demands to be met before he'll agree to leave."

Her stomach twisted into knots. Max should've just let her go. She was going to die anyway.

Sarah stepped forward, ready to offer herself up.

"But we won't give in to their demands," Rex

said, his eyes meeting hers for a moment as he looked around the room. "We fight."

Max pulled Sarah away from the crowd as Rex gave the last-minute plans. "You don't have to go out there, Sarah. No one expects you to fight your own father. We can put you in the safe room."

"I have to." She knew it as soon as she said it, and there was no changing it now. "I have to go out there; otherwise, I'll just keep hiding from this. That's what I've been doing: staying inside, trying to keep the kids close, and constantly watching. I'm not living. I'm just hiding. And the problem has caught up with me regardless. I have to fight, Max."

"All right." He glanced up to where everyone was taking their places. "Then let's go."

The next few seconds were a whirlwind as someone flung open the front door. Rex charged out first, tackling Edward head-on. The other Glenwoods streamed out behind him and onto the lawn, taking on the Greystones as they charged on the flanks of their leader.

Sarah felt her wolf rise up within her, eager and ready. She let it overtake her, welcoming the pain. It was nothing compared to all the suffering her father had put her through. Her bones cracked and her guts twisted. She felt the aching throb of her nails turning to claws, and the wind tunneled through her ears as they moved. Sarah nearly bit her tongue with her sharp fangs as she thrust herself forward onto all fours.

Carter faced her, his hackles up and his yellow eyes glowing. *You actually came out to fight for yourself?* he taunted. *What a fucking joke. At least it'll make my job easier.*

A chill rippled down her spine. The Greystones may have made her an outcast, but they couldn't sever the mental link that still existed between them. *I wouldn't be so sure of that.*

Sarah was fueled not by regular training or exceptional skill. She knew Max, Brody, and the others would be far better at this than she was. Her only hope was that it meant they wouldn't get hurt. As for her, she had no reason to care anymore. She hadn't been living, so did it really matter if she died? Not if she did so fighting for her children, the Glenwoods, or the life that had already been taken from her while she still breathed.

She launched forward, her teeth gnashing. Sarah aimed for his throat. Carter had been one of the men who'd captured her and returned her to her father. She remembered it clearly. He'd caught her by surprise, and she hadn't had a chance to fight him off. Things were different now. Her teeth caught in the thick scruff of fur beside his throat, and she clamped down hard.

Carter yanked back, snarling. He dragged her across the ground as he backed away, his claws scraping down the length of her belly as he tried to force her off of him, but Sarah only bit down harder. She knew she'd never get another grip on him like this. His blood filled her mouth and dripped off her muzzle. She had him.

Until he whipped his body to the side. The force was too much, and she lost her hold on him. Sarah flew through the air, her body completely out of her control, and slammed into the trunk of a maple tree. The air left her lungs, and the bark scraped against her hide. She fell to the ground, frozen.

You should've stuck with doing the dishes, Carter sneered. Blood dripped down his neck, staining his dark fur a deep burgundy. *Now I just have to decide if I'm going to finish you off myself or let Edward have the honor.*

He opened his jaws but snapped them shut again as a force impacted him from the side and he hit the ground. Hunter was younger and slimmer than his opponent, but his training made him a far better fighter. He didn't wait for Carter to recover from his

attack, bending down to quickly rip Carter's throat
and let him bleed.

Sarah watched the whole thing in horror, terrified for her son. *Be careful!*

I'm fine. Can you get up? He turned his back to her,
ready to defend her from the next strike.

The impact and surprise had knocked the wind
out of her, but Sarah found that her body was coop-
erating now. *I'm good. You need to get out of here. This
isn't your fight.*

*The hell it isn't! I was forced to grow up without a
mother because of these assholes.* Hunter looked off to
the right. *I think Conner needs help.*

Go! I'm all right. Sarah pushed herself to her feet
and shook out her fur. She may not have to fight
Carter anymore, but this battle was far from over. A
short distance away, she heard the terrified scream
of a wolf. She charged in that direction, ready to
help, but she stopped short as a ball of fire exploded
in the ground right in front of one of the Greystones.
Sarah looked back toward the house, expecting
Dawn or Joan.

Instead, it was Ava. She stood in her human
form, her hands and fingers working quickly as
wolves fought all around her. A blast went up just in
front of a Greystone guard, sending him reeling

backward. Frank charged at the girl, determined to be rid of the problem he'd been stuck with for so long. He had to pay for his arrogance when he ran forward despite the constant barrage from her magic. Dirt kicked up as a column of fire spouted up in front of him. There was no time for him to dodge out of the way.

There you are!

Sarah heard Gina's voice inside her head and instinctively dodged to the side. Her aunt's attack missed, but she easily swung around and came back for her. *I'm so sick of having to deal with you, you little bitch!*

I guess you don't have a choice now. Sarah felt her body tiring already. Even in wolf form, she wasn't ready for this. But she'd fight until there was no breath left in her if it meant a safe future for her children. She swerved to the side as Gina approached her again, looking for an opening.

But her father's sister was much more prepared for this than she was. She'd come at Sarah offset, like they were two knights in a jousting tournament. Just as Sarah thought she was about to pass her by, Gina thrust her paws into the dirt and shoved her shoulder into Sarah's side. Sarah crumpled to the ground, and Gina pounced.

Sarah fought to protect the most vulnerable parts of her body, but her aunt was everywhere. Her claws scraped and her teeth gnashed as Sarah squirmed beneath her. If she rolled over and got to her feet, she'd expose her back, and Gina would be all over her again. If she stayed where she was, she risked Gina getting a hold of her throat or ripping her belly open. Blood trickled through her fur.

As she struggled, Sarah's mind retreated from her body. She was back at the Greystone packhouse, but not as a captive. This was even longer ago than that, back when she was just a child.

"You're a meek little bitch just like your mother," Gina had said, a half-burned cigarette hanging out of her mouth. "I've never liked her, and I don't really care for you, either."

It was a ridiculous slight. It shouldn't even matter, considering Sarah hadn't been fond of Gina even before that time. But she was just a little girl.

The icing on the cake was the laughter she could still hear ringing through the living room after Gina's cackle: her father's.

Sarah returned to the present moment as though she'd fallen back into her body. A renewed energy flowed into her muscles, ignited by the way she'd been treated. She shoved her paws up into Gina's stomach. *You're my aunt! You should have looked out for me! You should have cared for me.*

Gina tossed her head back in surprise but quickly regained herself, twisting her head to the side and snapping her jaws too close to Sarah's throat. *You always were a whiner. That's fine. We'll take care of you and the rest of these freaks. We've got more silver collars at the packhouse for anyone left alive.*

Not if I have anything to do with it. Her claw raked through the thin skin near Gina's flank, sending out a warm spurt of blood. *You'll never do that to me or my children again.*

Gina moved her back paw, twisting away from the writhing wolf beneath her to keep the wound from tearing further open. *No, because we'll kill you and then we'll kill your Glenwood-spawned brats. I'll gladly do it myself. Slowly.*

Sarah shoved her back paw upward once again, thrashing against the open wound. Gina side-stepped, and Sarah saw her opening. She thrust herself upwards. It was her only shot. Her jaws closed around Gina's throat, and she yanked her head to the side.

"Stop!"

Sarah lay panting in a pool of blood. Gina was dead, as were several others, but there were still so many Greystones in the field adjacent to the pack-house. She had to get back up and keep fighting. She rolled to the side and hoisted herself to her paws.

"Stop!" the voice called out again, and this time Sarah recognized it as belonging to her mother. She watched as Janice walked into the field in human form. She held her hands clasped behind her back, completely defenseless. Sarah's heart lurched to see her there.

"As your pack Luna, I command you to stop fighting!" Janice lifted her chin as she strode through the field. Her shoulders were back, her eyes resolute as she moved toward the very center of the battle.

The Greystones paused, confused. The Glen-woods stopped as well, waiting. They watched her warily while keeping an eye on their erstwhile opponents.

Edward, in the center of the fray, stepped back from the Glenwood brothers and shifted back to his human form so that he could speak to her. "What the hell is this, woman?"

"I've come to put a stop to this," Janice announced. Her eyes met Sarah's for a brief moment before she looked back at her mate.

He laughed at her. "Are you kidding me? This

doesn't have anything to do with you. Go home where you belong."

"I won't." She lifted her chin higher. "Edward, what you've done is wrong. You've led this entire pack in the wrong direction simply because it suited your own purposes. You mistreated our daughter and granddaughter, and you forced everyone else to follow along with you lest they face the same consequences."

Sarah flinched as Edward moved forward toward his mate, putting his face in hers. His cheeks were red, and sweat dripped down his temples. "Is that so? What the hell do you think you're going to do about it?"

"This." Janice swung her arms out from behind her back, and Sarah saw she hadn't been holding them clasped after all. She held a silver alloy collar, which she now snapped around her mate's neck.

"What the?" He tugged at the metal, his round face now turning purple. "This isn't funny, Janice!"

"I never meant for it to be."

"As your Alpha, I command you to remove this at once!"

"I proclaim myself to be the *new* Alpha of the Greystone clan. Anyone who doesn't agree with this should step forward now." She waited, but no one moved. "Glenwoods, I can't apologize enough for my mate's repugnant behavior. Rest assured, this is where it ends."

Rex stepped forward and reached out for her hand. "Apology accepted, Janice. Thank you."

The battle was over as quickly as it'd begun. Sarah let go of her wolf. Her legs and feet were heavy. What she had just seen was reason to hope for the future, but she still felt the burden of all that had happened in her head and in her heart.

"Ava! Ava, come back to us."

Sarah's attention snapped to Max's voice. She saw him a short distance away, crouching in the grass next to Hunter. Somehow, she managed to get her feet to move. "What's wrong?"

"She decided to take on her wolf form and fight instead of just using her magic," Hunter explained.

Max ripped off the bottom of his shirt and pressed it to Ava's side, where blood was soaking into the ground. "She's bleeding too much. Ava, honey, you've got to get back into your wolf. You won't heal up unless you do."

Ava's eyes fluttered, and she tried to shake her head. "I can't. It's gone."

"Dawn! Where's Dawn?" Max demanded.

Joan had just come running up from the other

direction. "Inside. She went to check on the safe room."

"Let's go, baby." Max scooped Ava up into his arms and ran.

Sarah went after him. Her lungs burned and her muscles ached. She had no more energy to run or even to speak, but she went anyway. She'd been ready to sacrifice her life to ensure that her children would have a better one, but now...

Hunter flung open the door, and Max hurtled into the house. "Dawn!"

She raced into the living room just as Max laid Ava down on the floor. She wasted no time in asking what was wrong, instead falling to her knees next to her niece. She checked her pulse and looked at her injury. "She's lost a lot of blood. She doesn't have much time left."

A sob escaped Sarah's throat as she stood by, helpless.

Dawn moved her hands over Ava's injury and closed her eyes. She murmured something to herself, but Sarah couldn't understand the words. A green glow radiated down her arms and around her fingers, the light pulsing and vibrating as Dawn continued.

Sarah bent forward and put her hands on her

knees as bile rose from her stomach. She couldn't lose Ava. Not now. Not after all they'd been through. Not when it was finally safe to live again.

Dawn shook her head and repositioned her hands. "It's not working. There's too much damage."

"Let me help." Joan kneeled next to her. Her dress was torn, her curly gray hair wild. Ava's blood smeared her hands as she placed them over Dawn's.

Sarah clasped her hands together under her chin. She didn't know what to do, but she wanted to do something. She couldn't just stand there and let her daughter die.

But now Joan was frowning. "It's not enough. We can't do this on our own. Where's Lori?"

"I'm right here." She'd just come in through the backdoor, and she gasped when she saw the figure on the floor. "Oh my god! What can I do?"

"Selene is our only hope right now," Joan advised.

Sarah's hand pressed over her mouth as her sight blurred with tears. What they needed was a doctor, a hospital, a team of medical professionals who understood how shifters worked, not some fictional woman in the sky. Ava wasn't going to make it. There was no time.

Max stood and stepped back to make room for

Lori. He pulled Sarah in under his arm and pressed his hand to his temple as he watched.

Once again, Dawn and Joan invoked their magical powers. The green glow pulsed over Ava's wound. Now, Lori sat down on the other side of Ava and took her hand. She tipped her head back and closed her eyes. "Selene, the all-seeing eye of the night, she who can bring light into the darkness, we humbly pray for your help. One of our own is too close to the veil. Keep her with us. We ask that you use your almighty powers, turning back the clock as only you can so that our dear sister can stay in our world. Selene, please hear us."

"Selene," Dawn and Joan echoed, "please hear us."

Lori's shoulders stiffened, and her head twitched slightly, but still she kept a hold of Ava's hand. The green light continued to emanate from the other two women. The seconds slowly ticked by, and Sarah couldn't be sure of what was happening. She leaned into Max. They might not be together, but they were both parents. They were both seeing this horrendous thing happening in front of them.

But then Ava's eyelids fluttered. The blood was no longer dripping from the shred of Max's shirt that he'd placed over the wound. The magical glow died out, and the women took their bloody hands from Ava's body.

Dawn pressed her fingers to the inside of Ava's wrist. "She's coming back to us."

Another sob racked Sarah's body. "Can that really be?"

Lori stroked her fingertips gently over Ava's forehead. "Selene has blessed you, Ava."

Sarah didn't want to believe. She didn't want to feel hope if it was misplaced, only to be dashed once again.

But then Ava opened her eyes. "Mom?"

"I'm right here, baby." Sarah darted forward and cradled Ava's head in her lap. She covered her forehead in kisses and stroked her tangled hair. Joy and relief washed over her, but she continued to cry. She'd nearly lost her. She'd tried so hard to raise this dear girl in the best way she knew how. She'd fought as hard as she could against the horrific circumstances Ava had been born into. When the Greystones had come for her, Sarah had been willing to give them anything they wanted so that Ava might live.

In the end, though, it was Selene who had saved her.

17

MAX KNEW THE GLENWOOD PACKHOUSE BETTER THAN the back of his hand. Growing up, he'd played hide-and-seek in every nook and cranny of it. His heart had been broken, repaired, and broken again there. He shouldn't feel strange about leaving it since he had a home of his own now, a place he could have his own routines and habits.

But Sarah wasn't there. He wasn't sure she ever would be.

Max crossed the bedroom to the dresser and checked the drawers. He hadn't left any socks or pajama bottoms in there, but he was definitely leaving something behind. Sarah and Ava would remain at the packhouse. Max and Sarah had agreed it was best to take time apart, and there was no question that the pack would take care of them until they were able to get on their feet. Every question was answered, yet one continued to linger in his heart. Would there ever truly be a chance for them to be together? Or was he just fooling himself, using the idea of their eventual reunion to placate the pain in his heart?

"Can I come in?" Sarah stood in the doorway. Her eyes had been red and puffy for a solid two days after the battle with the Greystones. The swelling had cleared, but uncertainty still lived there.

"Of course. It's your place as much as anyone else's." Max didn't mean to sound so bitter, but he was sure he would, no matter how many times he tried. He'd found his mate, but he'd failed to keep her. Twice.

"Do you mind if I close this? I'd like to talk."

"Sure."

She shut the door gently and lingered near it, bracing herself on the trim. "I'm sorry."

Anguish had continually sliced through his heart over the last several days. Having the same conversation over and over again wasn't going to help. "I think we've both apologized enough for everything."

"Not for this," she insisted. Sarah pushed herself off the wall and came forward, putting herself in front of him to look up into his eyes. "I've apologized for a lot, and I'm sure there's plenty more that I'll still need to apologize for, but this is different."

Inside, Max stabbed the bubble of hope that rose in his chest. There was nothing left to hope for, and it was time for him to be realistic. "All right."

Sarah's chest heaved as she drew in a big breath. "I never understood why your pack was still so devoted to Selene. I thought she was just this bizarre old myth, a wolf shifter legend that was nothing more than a story that was being taken way too seriously. I mean, none of the other packs around here still cling to the idea of her. It was impossible for me to comprehend how grown adults in this day and age could just look up at the moon and believe a magical lady inside it would solve all their problems. It's like believing in the tooth fairy or Santa Claus."

An argument against that notion threatened on the back of his tongue, but he swallowed it. He was done arguing.

"Maybe I just didn't want to believe it was anything more than a story," she continued quietly. "After all, how can someone believe in something so much greater than themselves when they don't have anything like that in their life? How can someone feel that such an old, ideological tradition is

anything other than a cage when all the other traditions they've experienced have felt the same way?"
Sarah shook her head as she slumped onto the
corner of the bed. "Max, I feel like such an idiot."

"There's no need—"

"Yes, there is. I refused to see the value in something that you held so dear. I can't apologize to you
enough for that, especially after seeing what Selene
did for Ava. Our daughter would be dead right now
if it weren't for her. Everything the rest of us could
do wouldn't have been enough, but Selene stepped
in and just—" She held her hands up helplessly.
"She just fixed her. It was a miracle, and I'm so sorry
I was angry and frustrated with you over your faith
in her."

He could see just how miserable she'd made
herself over this. Max wanted to reach out, to stroke
his hand down her hair, to wrap her in his arms and
kiss her, to show her that he'd forgiven her. Given
their agreement, the best he could manage was, "It's
okay."

"It's not. I've been a horrible person," she
lamented.

"No," he corrected her quickly. "You've been
trying hard to find the right path for yourself despite
growing up around people who didn't love and care

for you, despite your father treating you like a villain in some fairytale. I appreciate your apology, but I can also understand exactly where you were coming from."

Sarah blinked up at him and rubbed her lips together. "Thank you for that. I guess I've had a hard time. I didn't think anyone really understood me."

"Maybe not," he confirmed. "Not in the way that you need to be understood, anyway, and that's what I need to apologize for. I've had my own burdens, but things have been much more normal for me, more stable. I thought I was trying to see things from your perspective, but I don't think I truly did until now."

She bent her head toward her clasped hands. "It's kind of funny, isn't it?"

"Hm?"

"That we can finally come to this point together, but not until after we've decided to split." Her words filled the room and then fell into a thick and heavy silence.

He'd been right. He'd been fooling himself. This was the last chance he might ever have. "I don't want to."

Sarah's head snapped up. "You don't?"

"No." His breath came quickly and his heart pounded, but he dared to step forward and take one of her hands in his own. "Sarah, I love you. I've wanted to be with you since the day we met, and I can't imagine walking out the front door and not leaving with you. I want to be a family with you, Hunter, and Ava. I want to know that even if we argue—because I'm sure we will—we'll figure out how to make it work."

She stood now, her fingers tightening in his. "And then we get to make up afterward."

He smiled as their lips met, and Max could feel himself falling for her all over again. She was new to him, yet she held a comforting familiarity. That was exactly how he'd felt when he'd first met her all those years ago. That was how fate worked, after all. It bonded them before they came to this earth so they'd always be able to find each other.

He abandoned himself to the velvet of her mouth, the way her lips melted into his. He delved his tongue inside, and her own tangled with it. Max felt his body tightening, his wolf reacting. There had never been any doubt that he wanted her, but this was so much more than that. A low moan reverberated up from her lungs and into his mouth, setting him alight with desire.

Sarah pulled back just enough to break their contact. "I've been thinking about something."

At some point during their kiss, he'd wrapped his arms around her. Now he traced his fingers along the curve of her backside, keeping her close. "What's that?"

"I've been wrong about a lot of things." Her breath whispered against his lips.

He shook his head and leaned in closer. "We've already been through all of that."

"I never liked the idea of being marked."

Max paused in pursuit of the next kiss.

"I thought it was barbaric, dated. Something that really wasn't necessary to prove that two people were mated." She lifted a hand and traced her fingers from his temple, down his cheek, and along his jawline as her eyes searched his. "I can see now that it's so much more than that."

He pressed his lips in a gentle kiss against hers. "What are you saying?"

She closed her eyes and angled her body even more toward his. "We've been apart for so long, Max. We've always known that we were fated, but I want it to be more than that. We have the chance not just to be together, but to experience that connection in the way it was meant to be. I love having your pack around us, supporting our family. I love the idea of everyone knowing we're together, a bond without question. I love *you*, and I want everyone to know just how much I do."

His eyes drifted down to that curve of flesh just below her neck, the one that had been tempting him for so long. Max couldn't explain the inherent longing he had to put his mouth there, but now it was stronger than ever. "Are you sure?"

She tipped her head to the side, giving him access. "I've never been more sure of anything in my life."

A sharp pain seared his gums as his canines descended. Anticipation built inside him as he bent his head, inhaling the sweetness of her scent. Grazing his lips across her skin, he pulled her tightly toward him and sank his teeth into her flesh.

Sarah gasped, but she clung to him as he left his mark. The gasp turned into a long, breathy moan as she sagged in his embrace.

Max pulled back and kissed the fresh wound. "You doing okay?"

"Yeah." She trembled against him, her breath ragged. "That was incredible."

"It didn't hurt?" His wolf surged within him, longing to complete their ritual, but he didn't want her to be in pain.

Sarah swallowed as she looked up at him. She

still clung to his back, but there was a strength in her fingers that hadn't been there before. "It did, but not the way I expected." The corner of her mouth quirked up. "I kind of liked it, actually."

With a growl of desire, he covered her mouth with his and plunged his tongue into her depths. He wanted to touch and taste every part of her, to know that she belonged to him down to her very soul. Even more, he wanted to feel that he belonged to her. His need overflowed within him as he cupped her backside, his hips thrusting forward so she could feel the hardness in his jeans.

"Max." Sarah ran her fingers through his hair and down the back of his neck. She lifted his shirt, forcing him to let go of her long enough to get the cotton over the top of his head so she could fling it across the room. She splayed her hands across his chest, smoothing her fingers over his muscles and skin, letting the pad of her thumb slide over his nipple. "I want you inside me."

"You know this is it, right?" He tugged at her belt, flinging the buckle open and snapping the thin leather band off her hips. Need billowed through him like a drug, barely held in check. "I've marked you. Once we do this, it's just you and me. Forever."

"I know." She traced her kisses down the side of

his neck and into the hollow of his throat as she opened his jeans. When he kicked them aside, she rubbed her palm against his hardness, only the material of his boxer briefs keeping them apart. "That's what I want."

Did she know just how crazy she drove him? Even if she did, Max wanted her to do it again and again. "So do I, Sarah. I've wanted this for a long time. Just like this." He'd freed her from her shirt and jeans now, and her skin heated the dark blue cotton of her bra and panties. Their bodies slid together as they stood there, exploring, touching, wanting. Max savored the anticipation of it, letting it build inside him as he kissed the swell of her breasts and teased his fingers into the waistband of her panties.

A short tug on the elastic of his boxer briefs, and he was nude before her. Max thought of scooping Sarah onto the bed, but she surprised him by sliding her body down the front of his until she was on her knees. His breath caught and froze in his throat as she took his hard length into her mouth, the heat of her tongue sliding along his shaft and swirling around his head. She paused and plunged down-ward again, her lips closing tight around him, driving him into such beautiful agony. Her hands skimmed the sensitive skin of his inner thighs as she stroked him. His muscles tensed, and all the blood drained from his head. Max reached out and caught his balance on the dresser.

It felt so good, and he could let her go on forever, but there was so much more that he wanted. Max reached down and pulled her upright, lifting her off her feet and onto the bed. He straddled her hips, fighting to restrain himself. He started on her shoulder, just shy of the fresh mark he'd imprinted on her. With his teeth, Max slowly slid down first one bra strap and then the other. It was excruciating to drag it out like this, but it was such an exquisite torture.

He dipped his tongue down into the cups of her bra to find her nipples already standing at attention. When Max slipped apart the clasp at the front of her bra and released her breasts, he thought he might come undone himself. Instead, he captured each in turn with his mouth, suckling and licking until it was his turn to work downward.

His mouth worked over the softness of her stomach and to each side. He nipped her hipbones and felt her squirm beneath his touch. The true treasure was just below. His pulse throbbed in his wrists as he pulled her panties aside and captured her heat in his mouth.

Sarah let out a strangled cry. Her body tensed, and he could feel her trembling all over again. She twisted the covers in her fists as he laved his tongue along her delicate folds, lingering on her tight bud and driving harder when her hips bucked against him. Every ounce of her pleasure was his own, growing to an intensity he'd never known. As he slipped his thick fingers inside her, he felt pulses radiating through her core. Sarah threw her head back, panting.

Max held tightly to her hip with his other hand as her orgasm intensified, devouring her. She pulled back when the spasms slowed, but he wasn't done yet. He worked her over with his mouth, touching her, tasting her, driving her, and she pounded her fist into the mattress. Nothing was more beautiful than seeing her writhing on the waves of his attentions. Max drew her further into his mouth and flicked his tongue in figure eights, knowing she was nearly at her peak. He could feel it within her and wanted it for both of them. Sarah snatched a pillow and screamed into it as her hips thrust into him again.

He could stand no more. Max lightly nipped her inner thigh before raising up onto his hands and knees. He pressed himself against her wetness as he looked down at her. She was glorious, her eyes shining, her lips plump and pink. Sarah gave him a desperate nod, urging him on, and he slid into her, melting at just how amazing she felt.

Their hips moved in unison as they rocked against each other, and her legs closed around him, burying him even deeper. Max moaned as he fully surrendered himself to the luxury of her softness and desire. The power of their love and connection swept over him. When he felt her tense up, ready to hit her apex, there was no need to hold himself back.

This was where he was meant to be—where they were both meant to be. As long as they were in each other's arms, nothing else mattered.

18

SARAH STEPPED INTO THE KITCHEN, A PLACE SHE'D slowly become familiar with all over again. The glasses and plates were still kept in the same cabinets as when she'd come to stay with Max before. The snacks hadn't moved, either, nor had the stash of chocolate. It was a small thing, but it'd been a comfort for Sarah to know that some things don't change, no matter how long you go without experiencing them.

This was a room full of magic, but not the same kind Ava was learning. It was a place of gathering and discussing, of late-night planning, of hashing and rehashing. The Glenwoods had an official meeting room, but so many times, she'd seen them come together right there around the table. This was a place of belonging.

She laughed at herself for being such a sentimental fool, but the night before with Max had made her emotions run a little deeper. Sarah rubbed her arms as she checked each of the kitchen chairs. The evening had gotten cool, though her thoughts were still ablaze with the fire Max had ignited in her. She glanced through the pegs near the back door, finding plenty of random flannels and hoodies, but not what she was looking for. That man knew all the right places to touch her, both physically and emotionally. Fortunately, there would be many more chances for that in the future.

Just about to give up and go check another room, Sarah turned and spotted a cake in the center of the kitchen table. She hadn't really noticed it at first. Curious, Sarah stepped closer. It was covered in chocolate frosting, textured along the sides to make it look like bark. The top held her initials and Max's inside a heart, carved into the frosting as though they were carved into a tree. Warmth moved through her at seeing such a sweet gesture.

The very culprit stepped into the kitchen. His eyes danced when he looked at her, and she could feel her wolf responding to his. They'd always been close, but not like this. The mark had made it so, and she felt his pleasure as he stepped up next to her and looked down at the cake. "That's quite a masterpiece."

"It was very sweet of you. Did you make it yourself?" Max was a man capable of many things, but she'd never noticed him spending much time in the kitchen.

"Me?" He stepped back and looked at her sideways. "I've been out with Brody all morning discussing improvements to the defense of the packhouse and property. I thought you made it."

Sarah shook her head, puzzled. "Nope. I just came in here and saw it sitting there. I was looking for my sweatshirt, and Ava said she thought she saw it in here."

Max narrowed his eyes. "Hunter saw me come in and said the kitchen sink was leaking."

It took only a quick check to see that the sink wasn't leaking at all. She slowly looked back at Max and pursed her lips. "I think we're being parent-trapped."

He let out a snort of laughter. "Really?"

"Oh, yeah." She tapped her fingers on the counter, reviewing it all in her mind. "We'd told them we were going to take some time apart and that you and Hunter would be going back to your place. They've been getting along great, and they have a chance at having a complete household for the first time in their lives. I think they're trying to get us back together because they don't know we already are."

"They could've just talked to us," Max reasoned.

"Right, they could've just talked to two stubborn, hard-headed adults who would want nothing more than to listen to what a couple of teenagers had to say about love and fate," Sarah returned. "I'm sure that would've gone over beautifully."

Max bit his lip. "If they want to play games with us, then I say it's only fair we return the favor. Hunter! Ava! Come to the kitchen, please!"

She wiped her hand over her mouth, trying to keep herself from laughing as the two teens came racing into the kitchen. It was adorable that they had gone to so much effort, even if it wasn't necessary.

"What's up?" Ava asked. She'd come in a little behind Hunter, having a bit of recovery yet from her injury, but her grin split her face. "Did you find your sweatshirt?"

"I didn't."

"And I didn't find a leaking sink, either." Max folded his arms in front of his chest and gave their son a stern look. "I think it's about time the two of you told us what's going on here."

The kids shared a look. Ava fidgeted as she looked down at the floor. "Hunter and I talked after you guys told us you weren't staying together, and we didn't think it was right. I mean, you're fated. Everyone knows it, and I think everyone can see it."

Hunter scratched the back of his neck. "We thought that maybe if you saw the cake and thought about it a little, you'd change your minds."

Sarah sighed. "Guys, I know it all seems simple to you, but these things can't be forced. You can't always make things work just because you want them to." It was a lesson Sarah felt she'd certainly learned herself. It wasn't until she and Max were able to step back a bit from their relationship and see it from a different angle that they'd truly figured it out. Trying to force themselves to be what they were 'supposed' to be hadn't been the right way to approach it.

"But we really do want it to work out," Ava pleaded. "I mean, the packhouse is nice and all, but I think you'd have a much better chance at a relationship if we were all in one house together. You know?"

"And just think about how much I'll be able to help Ava when school starts up. I can give her a tour of the high school, and I can even drop her off in the mornings," Hunter added.

Damn. They were making this hard.

Max was holding out better than Sarah was. "Manipulating us isn't the right way to go about it."

"I know, and we're sorry, but—wait." Ava pointed at Sarah's neck. "What is that? Is that what I think it is?"

Sarah knew she was caught, and she laughed as her daughter stepped forward and tugged at the collar of her shirt. "Yes, okay? It's exactly what you think it is!"

"Yes!" Hunter threw his fists in the air. "I knew it! You tried to trick us!"

"Only because you tried to trick us," Max pointed out. "I'm glad you wanted us to be together, but you could've just let us know how you felt."

Ava was screaming and jumping up and down. "Well, now you know! And so do we! This is great! I can't believe it!"

"Does this mean you're going to move in with us?" Hunter asked.

Max put his arm around Sarah's waist. "It does."

"Grandma!" Ava went running down the hallway. "Mom and Dad are moving in together!"

The joy that filled Sarah's heart overflowed at

hearing Ava refer to Max as her father. He was, and she'd never had any reason to feel otherwise, but it solidified everything she'd ever wanted.

"What the hell is going on in here?" Rex asked as he came in. "I was working in my den, but I can't even hear myself think over all this screaming."

"It's Dad! And Mom!" Hunter tripped over his own tongue, trying to get it out. "They're back together."

If she thought she was touched before, it was nothing compared to hearing Hunter call her Mom. They'd all been carefully avoiding such things, but now there was no reason. She pulled Hunter into a hug. It caught him off guard for a second, but then he hugged her back.

"I'm not surprised." Rex clapped Max on the shoulder. "Is that what this cake is all about?"

Max laughed. "I guess it is."

Ava came back into the kitchen, dragging Joan along behind her. "Come and see!"

Joan laughed. "I can see, sweet girl. I can see. We've had a lot of reasons to celebrate lately, and I'm more than happy to do it all over again. Now let's cut that cake!"

Sarah opened a cabinet to get a stack of dessert

plates. She felt a pair of strong arms wrap around her waist, and she leaned back against him.

"I think it's safe to say that everyone approves." Max's voice was a deep rumble near her ear.

She set the plates on the counter as she listened to the others in the room carrying on. "Were you worried?"

"No." He kissed her temple and then let go of her so he could pick up the plates. "I was much more worried they'd be upset with me if we weren't together, actually."

Ava and Hunter were still exclaiming over this change, and Joan and Rex were patiently listening. As Sarah joined them at the table, she decided Max was right. It was as though this family had always known what would happen; they just had to wait for the right time. She looked at Max, serving up a piece of cake to his mother, joking with his brother, laughing with his children.

He was worth the wait.

19

"Get those plates out onto the table."

"Did you see where I put the napkins?"

"Please tell me Rex already has the burger patties made up. We're running short on time."

The Glenwood kitchen was complete chaos as everyone scrambled to get ready. The extra picnic tables had been pulled out of the garage the day before, and Max had given them a thorough once-over with the pressure washer. Hunter had ensured the lawn was mowed and trimmed, although he grumbled about it along the way. Ava had planted new flowers in the big pots on the back porch. Jimmy had even put most of his automotive tools away and pushed his current restoration project to the back corner so the Glenwoods and their guests could easily grab drinks from the fridge in the garage.

"What else do we need to do?" Sarah captured her lower lip in her teeth and knitted her brows together as she looked over the backyard.

Max put his arm around her. "Honey, I don't think there's much else we *can* do. It's perfect."

"I don't know." She leaned into him, but he could feel her practically vibrating with nervous energy. "There's got to be something I'm missing."

Knowing it would make her feel better, Max took a look around for himself. Dusk was upon them, casting a deep red-gold light on the property. Strings of bulbs zigzagged over the tops of the picnic tables, which were already laden with food even as more was brought out. Soft instrumental music came from speakers set up in the eaves of the porch. Rex and Brody stood at the grill, arguing over when the meat should be taken off. Between the two of them, there was no doubt the meal would be incredible. The Glenwoods liked their barbecues, but this was more trouble than even they usually went to.

"I really can't think of anything," he said honestly. "It looks perfect, and so do you. I like that shirt on you."

Sarah looked down and then back up with horror in her eyes. "I've got to go change my shirt!"

"What's wrong with the one you're wearing?" The soft fabric of the t-shirt clung nicely to her curves, and Max liked the way it felt under his hands.

"This is the one I've been cooking and sweating in," she explained quickly. "I brought a different one with me. I'll be right back."

"Okay." He watched her go running back into the house.

Brody set a platter of pork steaks on the table and smiled at his brother. "I'd say she's a little nervous."

"I can't blame her." Max took another look at the back door Sarah had just gone through, even though she was probably already in the downstairs bathroom, changing her shirt and checking her hair and makeup. She wasn't the type to worry about making sure she was dressed up just to run to the grocery store, but he knew she wanted to make a good impression. "This is a big deal for her."

"It is for all of us, really." Brody stepped up onto the porch and flicked a switch, turning on the lights that'd been strung over the party area. "We've never had anything like this happen in the history of our pack, or at least not that I know of."

Max felt the conflicting emotions over that deep within him. "It's not right that it's had to come at such a cost."

Brody nodded. He knew what Max meant. None of them were happy to know what Sarah and Ava had gone through, even if the end result was such a good one. "I know. How are things going with having double the people at your place now? Is it driving you crazy yet?"

Max didn't mind the change in subject. "Crazy in the sense that Ava has suddenly figured out what shopping is and wants to do it all the time, yes. We've been to every store in Eugene at least twice. But I'm not complaining. There's nothing better than seeing her happy. And then Sarah looks at her, and *she's* happy, and then I'm happy all over again."

"And Hunter?" Brody continued. "I know how excited he was to have a little sister, but you know how kids are. That sort of thing can wear off fast."

It only took a slight turn of his head to see the siblings near one of the tables, arguing over who would get to sit where. "They fight like cats and dogs. Hunter thinks he knows everything and wants to impart his wisdom. Ava gets annoyed and uses her magic to irritate him. But then you look at them five minutes later, and they're playing video games or asking to go to the movies. They're good."

"I'm happy for you, man." Brody clapped him on the shoulder. "I'm also happy for me because you're a lot less dark and moody these days. It makes you easier to get along with."

"Kiss my ass." Max gave him a light punch in the arm.

Joan came to stand beside them. "Boys, I think it's about time."

Max hadn't been paying attention, but his wolf was instinctively on alert. He told it to calm down, reassuring it that everything was okay, but it wasn't easy as several pairs of eyes appeared in the darkness of the tree line. They moved easily but slowed as they reached the yard, leaving their wolves behind and coming forward in human form.

Sarah came out of the house and stood next to Max just as Janice arrived. Max could feel her fidgeting nervously with her shirt and bracelets, chewing her lips with anticipation.

Janice gave her a sweet smile, but she first came to Rex, who stood waiting. "I, as Alpha of the Greystones, officially extend an offer of peace. It is our desire that we have goodwill and community between our packs in a true alliance."

"Janice Greystone." Rex could be a very casual man, but when he performed his duties, he took on a stern and somber attitude. He now stood tall and proud in front of his equal. "I, as Alpha of the Glenwoods, do humbly accept your offer and extend the same. We ask that you dine with us to solidify this alliance."

"We accept."

With a nod from each of them, it was official. Glenwoods and Greystones filtered in from all directions to eat, drink, and finally get to know each other.

Janice, however, came to speak with her daughter, a small dog following along at her heels. She gave Max a smile, but her face softened entirely when she looked at Sarah. "Hello, my dear."

"Mom." Sarah wrapped the older woman in her arms and rested her head on her shoulder. "Isn't this incredible?"

"Yes, it is. And so are you, my dear." Janice pulled back to hold her daughter at arm's length, looking her all over. "I can see that this is working out wonderfully for you. I don't think I've ever seen you so happy."

"That's because I haven't been." Sarah looked at Max, her face sweet and content. "This is how it was always meant to be."

"Yes, I know." Janice's mouth trembled a bit as she let go of Sarah and looked at Max. "While I know the official reason for our visit here tonight is to create an alliance with your pack, I've also come on a personal mission. I owe you both an apology. Max, I'd first like to apologize to you. My husband didn't like the idea of Sarah being with someone he thought had a contaminated bloodline. It was a ridiculous notion and one that I never agreed with. I should have stood up for you all those years ago when I could see just how much you meant to Sarah and that the two of you were destined to be together. I can't even begin to tell you how much it saddens me to know that I was the least bit involved in keeping the two of you apart."

Max saw all the pain behind her words. Her inaction had caused a lot of similar pain in himself, in Sarah, and in their children, but he knew it was only due to her fear of Edward. It was time to move forward with their lives. "You're forgiven."

She clasped his hand and squeezed it tightly. "Thank you."

"Of course."

"And Sarah. Oh, my dear, sweet Sarah. I can't even begin to tell you all of my regrets." Janice turned back to her daughter, holding back tears.

"Mom, you don't have to," Sarah replied. "I know what it was like. I lived through it just as you did."

"That's kind of you, but you're wrong. Your father is a horrible man, and he never treated you the way he should have. I was afraid of him for the longest time, and I let that fear keep me from doing what was right. I know that a thousand apologies will never be enough to make it up to you, but I hope that at least we can find a way to move on from here. I still want to be a part of your life, Sarah, and to know you and your family." She studied her daughter with concern and fear in her eyes.

"Mom, I know how he is. I understand. I always understood, and I knew that, in many ways, you were just as much of a prisoner as I was. You just had the illusion of freedom, even if it wasn't a reality." Sarah slipped her fingers into Max's and pressed hard, making her knuckles dig into his. "Can I ask what's been done with him?"

Janice nodded. "The only fitting punishment I saw was to make him live the same sort of life he forced you into for so long. He's very well guarded, and I can say that he's starting to see some of the errors of his ways."

"And there hasn't been any trouble with the rest of the pack?" Sarah asked carefully.

Max had been wondering about this as well. He'd been hopeful about Janice taking over as Alpha, but it'd been rather unexpected. The Greystones needed a strong leader, and they certainly deserved one.

This brought a small smile to Janice's face. "No, actually. The ones most loyal to him fought to their death in the battle. Those that remained were only following him out of fear, and there were far more of them than I ever would've realized. I knew that taking over the pack was a desperate act, but it's one I'm very grateful for."

"So are we," Max replied genuinely.

"Dad, can we start a bonfire?" Ava asked as she came over. "We found a whole bunch of marshmallows in the pantry, and Hunter said we have to try them over a fire. Oh, hi Grandma!"

"Ava." Janice pulled Ava close. "I'm so happy to see you. I'm so sorry you were hurt, but I'm glad you're all right now."

"Oh, yeah," Ava replied dismissively. "I'm completely fine."

"What a pretty necklace." Janice admired the moonstone at Ava's neck.

"Thanks. Grandma Joan gave it to me, and she said it'll give me blessings and protection from Selene. Do you know who that is?" Ava looked happy and excited to share her experience.

"I'm not too familiar with her, so you'll have to tell me more later." The little dog at Janice's feet darted forward, wagging his tail excitedly as he danced his front paws on Ava's feet.

"Gina's dog! You kept him! I was wondering what might've happened to him after we left!" Ava scooped him up and held him, wiggling against her. "I never did find out what his name was."

"I don't think Gina ever actually named him, either. I've been debating it myself. Do you have any ideas?"

"Um." She wrinkled her nose as the dog licked her chin. "I've been reading a lot about ancient Greek gods and goddesses lately. How about Argos?"

"Argos it is," Janice agreed immediately. "You can come and see him any time, or I'll be happy to bring him here."

"Hey!" Hunter jogged over, addressing Ava. "Did you ask Mom and Dad about the bonfire? Aw, who's this guy?" He held out his hand for Argos to sniff.

"The bonfire is fine," Max answered. He'd been enjoying watching them all interact so much that he'd almost completely forgotten about the question. There was a certain joy that came from hearing both of his kids refer to himself and Sarah as Mom and Dad, too. After such a long time of being estranged, it helped him know that they were truly together again. "Make sure any other kids who might want to roast marshmallows have what they need, too."

Hunter and Ava ran off with Argos at their heels.

"I should probably go speak with Rex for a bit while I'm here," Janice said, smiling as she watched the kids go. "I have a lot to learn about being an Alpha, and I sure didn't learn anything about it from Edward."

Max's hand was still entangled with Sarah's, and he tugged her toward him. "How are you holding up? I know this is a lot for you, and you were a bit nervous right before it all started."

"I was," she admitted as she slipped her hands around his waist. "Logically, I knew everything would work out, but there was still this little nudge of fear at the back of my mind. I imagine it'll be there for a while, but I'm working on it."

He kissed her forehead. "I don't want you to ever be afraid again."

"That'll come with time. Knowing that the Greystones are firmly in good hands will only help that, as well as the alliance with the Glenwoods. But don't worry about me, Max. I'm fine. I've got you and the kids, and that's all I really need. You know?"

He held her tightly against him. It was unbelievable just how much time they'd spent apart, longing for the other. They'd held on, hoping and waiting, and it was all worth it. He had his mate back, the one woman he wanted in the entire universe, and she looked up at him with such desire and contentment in her eyes. His kids were a short distance away: the son he'd been raising and the daughter he was overjoyed to meet.

Both of their packs surrounded them now, and Max felt his life was finally complete. "I do."

THE END

If you enjoyed Max and Sarah's story, read on for a preview of Dawn and Gage's story, *Rejected Midlife Wolf*!

DAWN

"We've got one coming in on the ambulance. It sounded like a bad one over the radio. Animal attack of some sort."

"Really?" Dawn's heart pounded as she finished cleaning up and pulled on a fresh set of gloves. Her wolf was on high alert as she followed Nicki to the back of the ER. She knew that animals didn't just attack people, at least not most of the time. The same fears that had driven her into the medical field in the first place also made her job far more difficult.

The doors burst open as the paramedics raced in with the gurney. "He's bleeding badly. Unconscious. Looks like he was ripped apart by something."

Dawn's eyes scanned the pressure bandages that'd been placed on him just to keep him together.

There wasn't a single thread of them that wasn't soaked with blood. "Vitals?"

"Not good. His BP keeps dropping. We worked on him the whole way here, but we couldn't do much more."

"Name?" She grabbed her flashlight and moved up toward his head while several more doctors and nurses came crowding in. This was a bad one, and it was going to take a team. Dawn was about to check his eyes and see if he could hear her, but as she stepped toward his head, she paused.

Blood dripped from a wound near his scalp, and one eye was quickly swelling shut. He was older now, with gray dotting the stubble along his jawline, but Dawn would recognize Gage Edwards anywhere.

Her mind flashed back to a crisp October day, and the pain stabbed through her heart all over again. She'd been so hopeful. What the two of them had could've been so right, and she'd only wanted to make it better. His angry words echoed in her mind, his face twisted with hatred.

"Dawn? Earth to Dawn…"

She fell back into the present, sure that she'd been gone for only a moment, and looked up at Nicki. "Yeah. Sorry."

"Some lady found him on the side of the road

like this," the paramedic supplied in response to her earlier question. "All we have is what was on his license, Gage Edwards."

No matter what she knew about him, she had a job to do. In fact, it was *because* of what she knew about him that her job was all the more important. Shifters were everywhere in the Eugene area, but the vast majority of the humans around there had no idea they existed. It was her duty to make sure no one caught on to Gage's true identity.

That meant she had to pretend she didn't know a damn thing. Dawn reactivated herself, willing her body to fall into the typical routine of a trauma patient. She checked his pupils and frowned. "Mr. Edwards? Gage? Can you hear me? Move your fingers if you can hear me."

Nothing happened.

The paramedics got out of the way and onto their next emergency, leaving them to their job.

"Let's get him stitched up," commanded Dr. Hoffman. Dawn hadn't even been aware of him coming in. "I don't think he's got any internal bleeding. We need plenty of scans, but we can't do that while he's dripping everywhere. Nicki, start cleaning. Dawn, get that magic needle of yours. You start on his right, and I'll work on his left."

"Yes, doctor." Dawn's wolf was going wild now, and the adrenaline rushing through her system wasn't making things any better. Her hands were shaking as she prepped her sutures. Shaking hands were the last thing she needed right now.

She snagged a rolling stool with her foot and pulled it close. Her favorite professor in nursing school had told her long ago that the first rule of doing anything was to get comfortable. Most of the other students had laughed at the idea. Dawn had some doubts about it herself at the time. If there was an emergency, how was there time to get comfortable?

Years of experience had taught her otherwise. This patient would require a hell of a lot of stitches, and she wouldn't be able to do them as well if her back was straining or her feet were hurting. She jumped in at the first wound Nicki had finished cleaning, checking first for any damage to major blood vessels. Dawn knew she needed to work fast. She took a long piece of monofilament and went for a continuous stitch. It wasn't as sturdy as tying individual sutures, but there wasn't any time to get fancy. Besides, Gage didn't look like he'd be on his feet any time soon.

The next couple of hours went by in a blur.

Dawn worked quickly to help close up the wounds, and she stayed by his side as he was given several scans. Her muscles tensed, constantly worried that some slight difference in his physiology would give him away, but the ER staff wasn't looking for a shifter. They were just trying to keep him alive.

Finally, when it was well past midnight and getting close to the end of her shift, Dawn and an orderly brought him to ICU. Someone else could've done it, but she wasn't going to risk it.

"Oof. This guy's rough." Isaiah pushed the button on the elevator.

Dawn gave him a side-eye. "You've worked here long enough to know better than that."

"But you said he hasn't woken up since he's been here," the orderly countered.

She pursed her lips. It was true, and it wasn't good. He could be out of it for a long time, considering the injuries he'd sustained. None of the doctors who'd looked him over were particularly hopeful about his recovery. All they could do was wait. "You never know. He might be able to hear us."

"Then maybe he'll wake up and tell us what happened to him. He looks like he got attacked by a monster or something."

Dawn chewed her lip and willed the elevator to

hurry the hell up. She knew exactly what had happened to Gage, even if she didn't know the circumstances. Those wounds were all too familiar. "Yeah. Something."

Finally, the elevator slowed, and the doors opened. Tammy, one of the ICU nurses, guided them into the room at the end of the hall. "I think we're good to go," she announced after she'd ensured all the machines were running efficiently.

"I'd like a minute with him, if you don't mind." Dawn looked down at Gage, or at least the man she knew as Gage.

"Oh." Tammy's forehead wrinkled. "Do you know him?"

"Old acquaintances." It was the easiest way to explain it, even though it wasn't accurate. Dawn still felt that same fated pull, that tugging of her soul. Isaiah had been right, even though he'd been kind of crass about it. Gage was in rough shape. Every doc that had looked at him had clucked their tongues or shaken their heads. There was only so much they could do, and none of them expected him to make it.

Dawn swallowed. She had gone through all the required schooling to be a nurse, and there was a lot she could do with the same medical equipment that a human would use. As the Glenwood pack healer, she had something else in her arsenal, though, something that would be frowned upon if anyone else in the hospital knew about it. Could she get away with it?

Her wolf urged her on, consequences be damned.

"Okay. Let's see what we can do." Dawn took a cursory look around the room before shaking out her hands and placing them on his chest. She tipped her head back and closed her eyes, sending her energy toward him. Warmth radiated from her chest, down her arms, and into her fingertips. She felt it sinking into him, and in her mind's eye, she could see the green glow others had told her about.

Her magic was strong, she knew, but Gage needed everything he could get. "Selene, please hear my prayer. Bring him back from the brink he hangs on. He's swaying between worlds right now, between night and day. Push him back to me. Give him back the life he was meant to live."

Though her powers were strong, they drained quickly when she put them to work healing. The warmth faded, and she opened her eyes. Everything was as it was before. No one had seen a strange light and ran into the room. His vitals were stable, but no great miracle had happened. He lay placidly in the bed, the machines beeping away around him.

"Well, I tried," Dawn said with a sigh. "If you really can hear me, I'll probably regret saying this, but you still look just as hot as you ever did, even though you're all beat up. You may hate my guts, Gage, but eventually, you're going to wake up and tell me what the hell happened. You don't owe me anything, but I did help save your life. I think you at least owe me that."

Her eyes scanned his face, down his neck, and across his chest. A sheet covered everything else. Dawn had been working in the medical field long enough to see bodies of all types. Gage, though. Gage was different. She'd hardly paid attention while she'd whipped her needle through his wounds to keep him from dying, but now her curiosity was up. He'd always had a great body. Was everything just as appealing as it always had been? She knew it was wrong, but her wolf urged her to find out.

She glanced at the door and then lifted the top of the sheet. His chest was wide and strong, the muscles even more developed than they'd been all those years ago. They descended into rippling abs, so he'd definitely been keeping in shape all this time. A trail of curls started just below his navel, leading to—

"Dawn?"

Snapping up her head and dropping the sheet, Dawn gasped when she saw those deep brown eyes looking into hers. "Gage."

———

ALSO BY MEG RIPLEY
ALL AVAILABLE ON AMAZON

Shifter Nation Universe

Marked Over Forty Series

Fated Over Forty Series

Wild Frontier Shifters Series

Special Ops Shifters: L.A. Force Series

Special Ops Shifters: Dallas Force Series

Special Ops Shifters Series (original D.C. Force)

Werebears of Acadia Series

Werebears of the Everglades Series

Werebears of Glacier Bay Series

Werebears of Big Bend Series

Dragons of Charok Universe

Daddy Dragon Guardians Series

Shifters Between Worlds Series

Dragon Mates: The Complete Dragons of Charok
Universe Collection (Includes Daddy Dragon Guardians
and Shifters Between Worlds)

More Shifter Romance Series

Beverly Hills Dragons Series

Dragons of Sin City Series

Dragons of the Darkblood Secret Society Series

Packs of the Pacific Northwest Series

Compilations

Forever Fated Mates Collection

Shifter Daddies Collection

Early Novellas

Mated By The Dragon Boss

Claimed By The Werebears of Green Tree

Bearer of Secrets

Rogue Wolf

ABOUT THE AUTHOR

Steamy shifter romance author Meg Ripley is a Seattle native who's relocated to New England. She can often be found whipping up her next tale curled up in a local coffee house with a cappuccino and her laptop.

Download *Alpha's Midlife Baby,* the steamy prequel to Meg's Fated Over Forty series, when you sign up for the Meg Ripley Insiders newsletter!

Sign up by visiting www.authormegripley.com

Connect with Meg

amazon.com/Meg-Ripley/e/B00Z8I9AXW
tiktok.com/@authormegripley
facebook.com/authormegripley
instagram.com/megripleybooks
bookbub.com/authors/meg-ripley
goodreads.com/megripley
pinterest.com/authormegripley

Printed in Great Britain
by Amazon

43430232R00148